Loveswept® 578

Charlotte Hughes
Island Rogue

BANTAM BOOKS

NEW YORK · TORONTO · LONDON · SYDNEY · AUCKLAND

ISLAND ROGUE

A Bantam Book / November 1992

*LOVESWEPT® and the wave design are registered
trademarks of Bantam Books, a division of
Bantam Doubleday Dell Publishing Group, Inc.
Registered in U.S. Patent
and Trademark Office and elsewhere.*

*If you would be interested in receiving protective vinyl
covers for your Loveswept books, please write to this address
for information:*

> *Loveswept
> Bantam Books
> P.O. Box 985
> Hicksville, NY 11802*

ISBN 0-553-44239-2

Published simultaneously in the United States and Canada

*Bantam Books are published by Bantam Books, a division of
Bantam Doubleday Dell Publishing Group, Inc. Its trademark,
consisting of the words "Bantam Books" and the portrayal of
a rooster, is Registered in U.S. Patent and Trademark Office
and in other countries. Marca Registrada. Bantam Books, 666
Fifth Avenue, New York, New York 10103.*

**"When are you going to stop running, Ellie?"
Cutter demanded.**

She pushed against his chest, but something fluttered in her stomach when her palm came into contact with his sweaty skin. "Look, I've already told you—"

"I know what you told me, Ellie, but I don't buy it. You're a beautiful woman with your whole life ahead of you, and you can't just curl up and die because of something one man did to you."

She stared back at him, speechless as he spoke in a soft voice. He drew invisible circles on her wrist as he spoke, his touch mesmerizing her as much as his voice. "You don't understand—" she began.

"I understand more than you know. You don't hold the patent on pain, Ellie. Everyone gets knocked around in this life. But I'm here now. Let me kiss away that pain." Without another word he touched her lips lightly with his own. . . .

WHAT ARE *LOVESWEPT* ROMANCES?

They are stories of true romance and touching emotion. We believe those two very important ingredients are constants in our highly sensual and very believable stories in the *LOVESWEPT* line. Our goal is to give you, the reader, stories of consistently high quality that may sometimes make you laugh, sometimes make you cry, but are always fresh and creative and contain many delightful surprises within their pages.

Most romance fans read an enormous number of books. Those they truly love, they keep. Others may be traded with friends and soon forgotten. We hope that each *LOVESWEPT* romance will be a treasure—a "keeper." We will always try to publish

LOVE STORIES YOU'LL NEVER FORGET
BY AUTHORS YOU'LL ALWAYS REMEMBER

The Editors

I would like to dedicate this book, with love, to two of my favorite people—Janet Evanovich and Donna Schaefer, for always being there. I'm lucky to have you.

Also, I'd like to thank the people of Oda's Restaurant and Tavern for inspiring this book and for serving the best buffalo wings I've ever tasted!

One

"Why would a young, single woman want to leave a place like Savannah and come all the way out here to some godforsaken island?"

"I wonder what she looks like?"

There was a snort of disgust. "Well, we ain't never had no good-lookin' women on this island, so I wouldn't get my hopes up."

Cutter Beaumont took another pull from his chocolate-drink bottle as he listened to the men gathered at the scuffed beech-wood bar in his tavern. A brief but heavy thunderstorm had driven them inside. "You boys want a cold beer?" he asked.

A man named Dicker Henry nodded. "May as well. The morning is already shot to hell with this bad weather."

Cutter reached behind the bar and grabbed a clean mug. "Why are you boys so worried about what this woman looks like," he asked, "when y'all got fine women at home?"

"You've seen our women," a burly red-haired

1

man named Mozelle Freeman said. "And you still have to ask that question?" The men roared with laughter.

Cutter rubbed the stubble along his jaw and regarded the men with humorous black eyes. His hair was the same shade of black, falling well past the collar of his flowered shirt which had been tucked into a pair of torn and frayed jeans. His Sunday best, he liked to call them, so faded they had a cottony sheen to them. He had a craggy, unfinished look, a little rough around the edges. A straw hat, placed at just the right angle on his head, made him look like a character out of Jimmy Buffett's song "Margaritaville."

He straightened and tossed them a stern look. "Listen, about this woman we got coming. I don't care if she's plainer than a stovepipe, I don't want y'all giving her a hard time. I know she's not one of us, but what d'ya say we try and get along with her just the same?"

"What if we don't like her?" a shrimper named Otis Bentley asked. "What if she comes off acting like those uppity tourists you cart around on your bus in the summer, takin' pictures and leavin' all their litter behind?"

"We don't have to like her," Cutter said. He wasn't about to tell the man he was charging her twice the usual rent on the house she was to stay in; otherwise, they'd expect him to split it with them. "Besides, she's only going to be here a few weeks. Six or eight at the most."

"We don't like havin' strangers on the island, do we, men?" Dicker said. "Especially when we don't stand to benefit." The men nodded in agreement.

Cutter straightened and adjusted his straw hat, noting the stubborn expressions before him. How did folks expect the island *and him* to prosper if they continued to give visitors a hard time? "Okay, I didn't want to have to do this," he said, "but y'all leave me no choice." He reached behind the bar and pulled out a shiny metal star and pinned it to his floral shirt.

"Oh hell, he's done pulled out his badge," Mozelle said.

"That's right." Cutter cleared his throat and took on a look of authority, which wasn't easy for him, considering he hadn't shaved in three days and his shirt still bore the signs of the mustard stains from his famous suicide-hot chili dogs. "As sheriff and mayor of Erskine Island, I hereby order you bunch of ill-mannered degenerates to act like gentlemen when the new tenant arrives. You got that? And for those of you who've forgotten what a gentleman acts like, you can just take your cues from me." The men fell into hearty guffaws as Cutter turned to a battered black-and-white portable television and flipped the channel. "Now that we've got that settled, it's time for my show."

Still chuckling, the group ordered fresh drinks and prepared to be quiet for the next hour while Cutter watched his program. Everybody on the island knew Cutter Beaumont didn't budge from the Last Chance Saloon until he'd seen his daily rerun of *Miami Vice*, and it pleased him greatly when folks commented that he resembled Don Johnson. "Tell you what," he said when a commercial came on. "You boys be nice to that woman, and I'll throw a party for you when she's gone."

The men looked interested now. They were always looking for a good party, and nobody threw 'em like Cutter. Which is why they appointed him sheriff and mayor every time elections rolled around. The voting process itself only took five minutes, but Cutter threw one helluva party afterward. Only if he won, of course. And he always won. The islanders had decided a long time ago it was wise to vote for the man who owned the only saloon on the island.

Mozelle was just about to agree to the terms of Cutter's deal when they heard a high-pitched voice coming from the grocery store that was attached to the saloon. Cutter owned that, too, and paid one of the island women to run it for him.

"Where is he?" a woman's voice demanded.

Dicker Henry almost fell off his barstool. "Hell's bells, it's Clovis!" he cried. "She'll wallop me one good if she finds me here."

"Hide behind the bar," Cutter told him, hoping and praying Clovis wasn't sporting her pistol.

"Where is that sorry no-good fool I married?"

The men glanced up at Clovis, the looks on their faces so innocent, one would have thought she had just interrupted a lesson on Bible scripture. "You looking for someone, Clovis?" Cutter asked.

Hands on hips, the toothless woman stalked toward him. She was close to six feet tall and as broad shouldered as Cutter himself. Her hair was brittle from peroxide. "Don't give me no bull, Cutter Beaumont, or I'll tie knots in that lyin' tongue of yours. I know he's here. I'm gonna give you to the count of three to tell me where."

"You carryin' a gun, Clovis, honey?"

"I don't need no gun. I got my bare hands."

It was a sorry excuse for a boat, held together by rust and mud and Lord only knew what else.

Ellie Parks gripped the ferryboat's railing as the sputtering contraption slammed against the main dock on Erskine Island with enough force to rattle her teeth, almost tossing her overboard and forcing her to become fish bait at the age of twenty-eight. She had never been so glad to see land in her life. They hadn't gotten halfway across the bay before a sudden violent thunderstorm had rolled in and made Ellie question, not for the first time, her decision to come to the island.

Once the captain had unloaded Ellie's bags and placed them on the dock, a tall man with skin the color of milk chocolate hurried over to her. "Howdy, ma'am. You must be the lady from Savannah I heard was comin'." He stuck out a hand in welcome. "Name's Clarence Davis," he said. "I'm the deputy sheriff here. Welcome to Erskine."

Ellie offered the young deputy a timid smile as he pumped her hand enthusiastically. He was nice looking, dressed in a uniform of khaki shorts and shirt, both of which were so stiffly starched she was certain they could stand alone. "Ellie Parks. Nice to meet you," she said. "I don't suppose you have a taxi service on the island, do you?" She indicated her luggage with a slight nod.

Clarence Davis threw back his head and laughed. "No ma'am. The only person on the island with wheels would be the sheriff, Cutter Beaumont. Everyone else either walks or rides a bicycle."

Ellie realized Beaumont was also the man who was supposed to have the key to the house she was renting. "Mr. Beaumont is the sheriff?"

"As well as the mayor. You can find him up at the Last Chance Saloon servin' cold beer."

"He works in the saloon too?"

"He owns it. Not to mention the general store. And if you're interested in buying used appliances or furniture, he sells 'em out of his storeroom."

"Ambitious fellow," she said.

"Oh no, ma'am. Least not the Cutter Beaumont I know. Now let me get your luggage and I'll walk you to the saloon and ask him to loan us his Jeep so we can take your stuff over to the Simmses' house, where you'll be stayin'."

Ellie nodded as the man ordered a young boy to keep his eye on her luggage until they returned with the Jeep. "This here's my nephew Franklin D.," Clarence said proudly. "Named after Franklin Delano Roosevelt. My sister named all her young-'uns after great people so they would all grow up to be great people themselves. Franklin D. is the youngest. Just turned five." Ellie smiled and spoke to the boy, but he didn't reply. "He cain't talk, Miss Parks," the deputy told her, then motioned for her to follow him.

Ellie followed the deputy up a winding gravel road to where several white-frame buildings stood at the top of a hill, surrounded by tall shade trees. "You'll like the Simmses' house," he told her. "Lots of privacy. Mrs. Simms 'bout pitched a fit when she had to leave it. Her son put her in a nursing home on the mainland when she took sick."

Ellie tried to keep up with Clarence's long-legged gait as they closed the distance between the docks and the buildings where bicycles and motor scooters stood behind a warped, hand-lettered sign listing rental costs.

"Tell me," she said. "How can Mr. Beaumont be the sheriff *and* the mayor?"

Clarence shrugged. "I reckon 'cause he wants to

be." He stepped onto the small sun-bleached porch attached to the store and dragged the screen door open. "After you, ma'am."

Thanking him, Ellie stepped inside the musty-smelling grocery store. She had never seen so much stuff crammed into one room before. Not only did the store carry a large selection of grocery items, including fresh meat, but there was also fishing tackle, bait, and a small selection of clothing, shoes, and bathing suits. Ellie smiled as a bespectacled middle-aged woman glanced up from her stool behind an antique cash register, nodded once, then went back to reading the magazine in her lap.

"This way, Miss Parks," Clarence said, motioning for Ellie to follow him to the back of the store, where a closed door did very little to buffer the noise from the next room. "Must be another fight goin' on," he commented, as though it were not uncommon to find islanders in some sort of skirmish.

"A fight?" Ellie didn't try to hide her surprise.

"Happens all the time, ma'am. Nothin' to worry about, though. Nobody ever gets hurt much."

"But I thought the island was crime free." At least that's what she had read.

Clarence shrugged. "Ain't a crime unless the sheriff officially charges somebody. Which he never does. If someone does something he don't like, he makes 'em cut grass or wash his Jeep or bathe his dogs."

"His dogs?"

"Coon dogs. Cutter keeps a bunch of 'em at his place." Clarence reached for the door and pulled it open, then held it so she could pass through first. It took a moment for her eyes to adjust to the dim light. It was then that she spotted a man and woman struggling near the bar.

"Anybody want to bet on who's goin' to win?" one of the onlookers asked, calmly sitting at the bar sipping his beer.

"I got my money on Clovis," another man said. He reached into his pocket, pulled out several bills, and slapped them on the counter.

"What's going on?" Ellie asked the deputy.

He shook his head sadly. "I reckon Clovis done caught Cutter sellin' beer to her old man again. She doesn't approve of alcohol."

Ellie nodded as she tried to get a better look at the two. "Which one is Cutter?"

"The one Clovis is whuppin' up on."

Ellie managed to get a look at the man who seemed to be doing his level best to wrestle the big woman's arms behind her back. She caught a glimpse of an unshaved jaw, glittering black eyes, and the widest set of shoulders she'd ever laid eyes on.

"Okay, Clovis, that's enough!" Cutter said, having finally wrestled the woman against the bar and pinned her arms behind her. He was unaware of his new audience. "Now you get your fanny outta my saloon and don't come back till you cool that nasty temper of yours. You got that?" When the woman didn't answer, he shook her slightly. "D'you hear me, Clovis Henry? I'm gonna let you go this time, but you have to promise to leave quietly." The woman didn't so much as bat an eye.

"I wouldn't let her go," Dicker warned, having come out of hiding.

Cutter relaxed his grip on the woman. "Naw, she's calmed down now. Right, Clovis?" He released her.

"Yeah, I'm calmed down now," she said. Then, without warning, she whirled around and caught Cutter right smack in the jaw with her fist. The resounding crack made the onlookers wince. Cutter's feet flew out from under him and he landed flat on his back on the unpolished plank floor.

Clovis dusted her hands with the satisfaction of one who'd just swatted a pesky house fly. She glared at her husband. "Dicker, are you comin', or am I going to have to bust you upside the head too?"

Dicker scurried from behind the bar like a frightened jackrabbit. "I'm comin', darlin', I'm comin'." He followed his wife out of the saloon, taking care to remain at a respectful distance.

"Okay, it's safe now," Clarence told Ellie, leading her closer to the bar where the injured man remained sprawled on the saloon floor like something out of an old Western film.

"Looks dead, if you ask me," Mozelle said, leaning over Cutter.

"He ain't dead," Otis Bentley said. "He's just playin' possum 'cause he don't want Clovis to come back and hit him again."

Cutter opened one eye. "Is she gone?"

Clarence stepped forward. "You're safe, Boss. Here, let me help you up." He offered the man a hand and hauled him to his feet.

Cutter staggered once, then blinked, waiting for his head to clear. "Lord, that Clovis really packs a punch," he said, running a hand across his throbbing, unshaved jaw.

The sight of blood caused Ellie to gasp aloud. "His lip is bleeding," she said, hurrying forward and reaching into her bag for a tissue. "Somebody get me some ice and a cloth. A clean one, if you have it," she added, though her tone was doubtful.

Cutter noticed the woman for the first time as she stepped closer and pressed a wad of tissue against the corner of his mouth, causing him to flinch. "Who are you?" he asked, the sound muffled as she applied pressure to his injury.

"Ellie Parks," she said.

"Boss, she's the one who's leasing the Simmses' house," Clarence told him. "Miss Parks, this here is Cutter Beaumont, our sheriff and mayor."

Ellie nodded at Cutter as a red-haired man handed her a cloth and a handful of ice cubes. "Thanks," she said, making an ice pack out of it and pressing it to Cutter's lip. The sight of blood still rattled her, which made her all the more determined to help the man. At the same time, she would have been blind not to notice that Cutter Beaumont had the sexiest set of lips she'd ever seen on a man, almost too full and sensual to belong to the opposite sex. She glanced up and met his black-eyed gaze, and her sense of discomfort worsened.

"Good thing for you you're wearing an old shirt," she said, trying to make her voice sound light, despite the fact that she suddenly felt confused and more than a little breathless. "You've got enough blood on it for three men."

The group of onlookers laughed. Cutter looked surprised, then a bit indignant. "This is the nicest shirt I own, lady."

Ellie blushed. "I'm sorry, I wasn't trying to insinuate there was anything wrong with it." She met his gaze once more. There was something about the way he looked at her. And he was standing much too close. "Here, you take this," she said, indicating the homemade ice pack. "If you can just hold it in place for a few minutes, it should stop the bleeding." She waited until he raised his hand to it before letting go, but not before he'd managed to brush her fingers with his. Ellie pulled back as though she'd been electrically shocked. She blushed again when she realized it had not gone unnoticed. Cutter's black eyes didn't miss a thing.

"So you're the one renting Martha Simms's house?" he said, studying the attractive strawberry blonde before him, who suddenly seemed as nervous as a polecat crossing a busy highway.

"Yes." Ellie fidgeted with her hands as she tried, once again, to meet his gaze. The men had resumed their places at the bar and seemed content to drink and talk among themselves now that it wasn't likely the saloon owner would bleed to death. "Your deputy offered to give me a lift. I just came by for the house key."

"Oh, he doesn't have to do that," Cutter said. "I'll drive you out personally." One corner of his mouth lifted in a funny half smile at the dubious look she shot him. "I figure I need to go home and change shirts anyway," he added, indicating the bloodstains.

Ellie knew she would feel more comfortable with his deputy who at least *resembled* a man of the law. "Oh, I hate to take you out of your way."

"It's not out of my way," he said. "Didn't Clarence tell you?"

Ellie looked from one man to the other. "Tell me what?"

"You and I are neighbors," Cutter said. "I own the land next door to the Simmses' place."

Ellie offered him the closest thing she had to a

smile. "Neighbors, huh? Imagine that." Frankly, she didn't know what to say. Surely it was to her advantage to live next door to the sheriff. What could be safer?

But then he smiled, a cocky, self-assured smile that was a little too bold, a little too intimate for her liking. It was the sort of smile lovers shared after a bout of good sex. It occurred to her then that the house next door to the sheriff might just be the most dangerous place on the island.

Two

By the time Cutter led Ellie outside to a yellow Jeep Laredo that looked as though it hadn't seen a washing in months, his lip had stopped bleeding and the swelling had gone down somewhat. Still, he was madder than a thirsty wasp in a drought, and as he drove the short distance to the main dock where Ellie had left her bags, he hinted at what he would like to do to Clovis Henry's person. His thoughts ranged from tarring and feathering her to tying large cement blocks to her size-ten feet and dropping her over the side of a fast-moving boat.

"Perhaps it would be best if you simply stopped serving alcohol to her husband," Ellie suggested, thinking the puffy lip gave him a rakish air. Not that he needed any help in that department. He already looked like the worst kind of rogue with his dark coloring and insolent manner.

"Let's get something straight, Miz Parks," he said. "I don't let anybody tell me how to run my business, especially some woman who won't allow

13

her husband to go off and have a little fun now and then. It's women like Clovis Henry who give marriage a bad name. Next to my ex-wife, that's the meanest woman I ever had the misfortune to run into."

Ellie had to smile at that. Cutter Beaumont sounded as though he'd had it up to his eyeballs with women. She couldn't help but wonder what his ex-wife had done to earn her meanest-woman-alive title. Whatever it was, Ellie was certain he had somehow deserved it. "Then if I were you, Sheriff, I'd get used to walking around with a sore lip because I think Clovis Henry means business."

Cutter snorted in disgust and parked beside the dock where Franklin D. was still sitting on one of Ellie's suitcases reading a comic book. While Cutter loaded her baggage into the back of the Jeep, Ellie thanked the boy and handed him a dollar bill. "Maybe you can buy yourself a new comic book," she suggested with a smile. The boy nodded, tucked the old one in his back pocket, and ambled away.

"Mind if I ask you something?" Ellie said to Cutter once they had climbed back into the Jeep. "What happened to Franklin D.'s voice? I understand he can't talk."

Cutter pulled onto the dirt road and started up the hill that led past the group of stores and his saloon. "The kid had a bad experience a couple of years ago." Cutter slowed the car and pointed. "See that pier over there? Franklin D. watched his older brother drown from that very spot."

Ellie sucked her breath in sharply at the thought. "Oh, how awful!"

"Yeah. It was hard on him. Franklin D. is smart

as a whip. But he hasn't so much as uttered a word in two years."

"Has anybody tried to help him?"

Cutter glanced at her. "What do you mean?"

"Like take him to a doctor? A child psychologist, maybe?"

Cutter offered her a patronizing smile. "These people don't hold much stock in shrinks, lady. Besides, the boy's mother says he'll talk when he's dern good'n ready."

Ellie wanted to say more, but she got the feeling Cutter didn't want to talk about it as he shoved a Garth Brooks tape in the tape deck and hummed along with the song, adjusting his straw hat so that it kept the sun out of his eyes.

She gazed at him as they bounced along a narrow, sandy road flanked by tall loblolly pines, snarled oaks, and flowering dogwoods. She could see that his hair, curling well past his collar, was as black as coal dust. Blue-black and silky, it looked as though it had been fashioned out of crows' feathers. His eyes, though they had appeared onyx in the dimly lighted tavern, were the color of Brazil nuts.

As though sensing her gaze on him, Cutter turned and found her staring. Another one of those smiles followed, the sort a man gives a woman when he has caught her looking and knows she likes what she sees. Ellie knew she was guilty as sin. She also knew it had been a long time since she had looked at a man, *really* looked. A scarlet stain crept up her neck and spread to her cheeks.

"Somethin' wrong?" he asked, his drawl as thick as syrup on a cold morning.

"I was just thinking that you don't resemble any

sheriff I've ever seen," she said, hoping he would think she'd been staring out of simple curiosity and nothing more. Instinct told her that Cutter Beaumont's ego didn't need any further stroking. With his looks, he was probably used to women gawking at him. "You don't even wear a badge or carry a gun," she added.

"I don't need a gun. We don't have any crime around here."

"What I saw in the saloon—"

"What you saw was a wife letting off a little steam. Not hardly worth making a fuss over now, is it?" He shrugged. "Besides, if I locked Clovis up, who'd watch after the children."

Actually, he wanted to kick his own behind for not ordering Clovis to clean up his Jeep. Not that he had the first clue how he would have enforced it, short of shooting the woman. But he was tired of driving around in a dirty vehicle. "You'll like the Simmses' house," he said after a moment. "Miz Simms kept things real nice. Even after she took sick, she paid one of the ladies from the Baptist church to come in and clean every week."

Ellie clasped her hands together in her lap as she listened. Her palms were damp. She was nervous. But it was silly to feel anxious around the man, she told herself. Even though he looked like the worst hood, as sheriff and mayor of Erskine he would have to possess a few scruples. She was simply going to have to get over the feeling that all men were out to hurt her. "Do you think Mrs. Simms will ever move back?" she asked, determined not to let her discomfort show.

Cutter shook his head. "No. She was using a walker when she left. Not only that, she was forgetful. It was getting to where I had to drop by several times a day to remind her to take her medicine and make sure she hadn't left a burner going on the stove."

Ellie watched him steer the car expertly along the narrow road, swerving to miss potholes and places where the road had washed away completely. She felt more relaxed knowing he was the sort of man who would take the time to see to the needs of an elderly woman. "Is she going to sell the place?"

"Why, are you interested?" Cutter tossed her a cocky grin, one that told her he wouldn't mind one iota if she decided to hang around. At the same time, the smile hinted that he was probably conceited enough to think he was the reason for her sudden interest in staying, despite the fact she'd known him less than an hour. When Ellie didn't bother to dignify the question with an answer, he went on. "No, Miz Simms isn't real keen on selling," he said. "She keeps thinking she'll get better and her son will let her come back. The only reason she asked me to rent it out was to help cover her expenses at the nursing home. But rental property isn't exactly in demand on Erskine," he added. Which is the very reason he couldn't figure out why Ellie Parks was there in the first place. He turned a corner and nodded toward a sprawling frame house. "Here we are," he said. "Good thing about living on this island, you don't have to go far to get where you want to be."

"Is that it?" Ellie asked, gazing at the rustic house that was partially hidden behind two flowering crab-apple trees. Two massive live oaks shaded the yard, each dripping with gray-green Spanish moss that made them appear noble and wizened. Mottled sunlight formed odd patterns in the lush ivy that hugged the ground beneath them. Ellie could feel the peace and tranquility flowing into her, and she was suddenly sorry for Mrs. Simms, who had been forced to leave this haven of comfort.

"That's it," Cutter replied as he pulled into a drive covered with oyster shells and flanked by dwarf crape myrtle. "See that line of pine trees over there? I've got me a double-wide on the other side. Bought it last year. You shoulda seen them trying to get it over on a barge."

Ellie was only half listening. She opened her door as soon as he pulled to a halt. "Oh, this is perfect," she said, hurrying across the yard.

"Grass needs cutting," Cutter pointed out. "I try to get someone out here on a regular basis. Miz Simms would have a fit if she saw how neglected her flower beds were."

Ellie noted the weed-infested flower beds as she made her way up the walk to a screened porch where an old metal glider rested along one side. She smiled, imagining herself spending a lazy afternoon there with a good book.

Cutter followed Ellie across the porch, but he was more interested in her at the moment than in his surroundings. Although she was a little on the skinny side, and a bit pale for his liking, he knew a few weeks on Erskine would change all that. Still, he couldn't figure out why a pretty woman like Ellie Parks would want to spend time on a remote island where the only entertainment was the video poker machines in his saloon and a big-screen TV for Monday-night football parties. Unless she was hiding from something or some-one.

"Here, let me unlock that for you," he said as

she stepped up to the door and peeked through the small window. He fumbled in his pocket for the set of keys he'd brought with him, then inserted one into the lock. He wiggled the knob, then shoved the door open. It creaked like something out of an old Hitchcock movie. "Hinges need oiling," he said.

Ellie stepped inside a neat front parlor and was surprised to find it so cool. No doubt the shade trees kept it that way. She noted the colorful rag rugs and sturdy furniture that had obviously been chosen for comfort instead of any aesthetic qualities. Still, it was cozy. She sniffed. "It's musty in here," she said, wondering how long the place had been closed up.

"Why don't I open a few windows while you look around?" Cutter offered.

Ellie explored the rest of the house while Cutter went from room to room opening windows so the place could air out. A quick inspection showed the house had three bedrooms, a small study of sorts, a bathroom with a claw-foot tub, and a large eat-in kitchen. The back porch held a washer that looked like it had come over with the first settlers.

"I think it still works," Cutter said when he found her looking inside the avocado green washing machine. "There's a clothesline out back. Miz Simms wouldn't buy a dryer because she claimed it would just be something else to break down on her." He paused and smiled as he thought of the elderly woman who'd once lived there. "As a matter of fact, she would never have allowed this washing machine had her son not bought it for her and forced her to use it. She preferred using her washboard in the bathtub."

"Were the two of you close?" Ellie asked.

He looked thoughtful. "Yeah, I reckon we were." He chuckled after a moment. "She was a strait-laced religious woman bent on saving everybody on the island, including me. She had this parrot she called Gabriel that I taught to cuss a little. One day when the preacher came to visit that bird cut loose with a bunch of four-letter words." He paused and laughed at the memory, and Ellie laughed with him. "I don't think Miz Simms ever forgave me for that one. Right before she took sick she was still trying to undo the damage by teaching Gabriel the words to 'Amazing Grace.' He'd mumble a chorus of it, then start cussing again."

They were still laughing as they returned to the kitchen, and for the first time Ellie felt completely at ease with him.

"Do the two of you keep in touch?" she asked.

He shrugged. "I've sent her a couple of postcards, but I'm not one for writing letters."

Ellie nodded. She couldn't imagine him being much of a letter writer either. She checked the old harvest gold refrigerator and found it empty except for a box of baking soda. "Guess I'll have to buy groceries," she said. "By the way . . ." She turned and found Cutter watching her curiously. Their gazes locked. Once again, she was reminded that they were all alone and that she didn't know a soul on the island.

"You were going to ask me something?" Cutter noticed the change in her immediately; facial muscles tensing, eyes taking on a cautious look. She crossed her arms, hugging herself tightly as though a sudden chill had stolen into the room.

She wondered what he was thinking, wondered what kind of man he really was. Did people ever really know what kind of person they were dealing with? Some people put on such a good front, it was difficult to tell what they were like deep down. Was Cutter Beaumont one of those people? she asked herself. "Uh, I was just wondering," she said. "Since there are no vehicles on the island, how do people get their groceries home?"

"Most folks live within walking distance of the store," he told her, "but me and my deputy don't mind giving anybody a lift if they need it. You'll notice a lot of people have baskets attached to their bicycles for just that purpose. I'll be glad to loan you one of my bikes from the store."

"What's the rent on them?"

"Ten dollars a day, but that's just for the tourists." He grinned. "I can give you a better deal."

She was tempted to ask him what he expected in return, but she didn't. Maybe he was simply trying to be friendly. Maybe she was reading more into it than he meant. Still, she couldn't imagine a wheeler-dealer like Cutter Beaumont giving anything without expecting something in return. "I doubt I'll need a bike. The walk back and forth will do me good."

"You don't look like you need the exercise to me," he said, his gaze roaming over her freely.

She stiffened. She didn't like the way he was looking at her. He was out of line. "Look, Sheriff—"

He could see that she was clearly nervous, so different from the girl who'd laughed with him only a moment before. "Call me Cutter," he said, trying to ease her sudden discomfort and lessen that grim set to her mouth. "And I'll call you Ellie. We don't hold much on formality around here."

"Perhaps you wouldn't mind helping me carry my bags in now," she said quickly. "I'm really tired, and I'd like to get settled."

"Tell you what," he said, stepping closer. "Seeing as you don't have any food in the house, why don't you come up to my place for dinner?"

Ellie regarded the man before her, one light brown brow arched quizzically. My, but he's a fast one, she thought. Fast, and smooth as polished cotton. He probably gave the island women a run for their money. "Maybe some other time," she said, although she knew it wasn't likely. She was there for peace and solitude, and Cutter would offer her neither. "I really am tired."

"I'm making a big pot of gumbo," he said, as though that in itself would tempt her beyond rational thought. "I'd hate to see it go to waste."

She smiled. "Try freezing it, Sheriff. It won't go bad."

He chuckled. "Why, Miz Parks, I'm beginning to think you don't like me."

"Don't be silly," she said. "I don't even know you." With that, she turned and made her way toward the front of the house. Cutter followed close behind. She was aware of his closeness, not because of the tangy scent of his cologne but because the skin on the back of her neck wouldn't stop prickling.

Grinning from ear to ear, Cutter beat her to the front door, stepped in front of her, and leaned against it so that it was impossible for Ellie to exit. "That can be rectified quick enough, you know."

Ellie came to an abrupt halt at his sudden appearance, but not before her thighs had managed to brush his. She stepped back. Something fluttered in her stomach. Her heart skipped a beat. "Please move out of my way."

He noted with an odd sense of curiosity the heightened color in her cheeks, the way her eyes darted constantly at the closed door. She was as jittery as a kitten stuck in a tall pine. "Listen, Ellie," he said softly. "I'm just trying to be friendly. There's not a lot happening on Erskine. We sort of have to make our own fun."

The words rolled off his tongue with the consistency of honey. "What makes you think I'm looking for fun?" she asked. "I simply want to be alone."

"What are you running from, Ellie?"

The way he said her name, like a caress, sent a shiver up her spine. Without warning, he stroked her bare arm, and she jumped, then tried to still her racing heart by placing a hand over her chest. But how could she be calm when he was standing in her way, blocking her passage, *trapping* her? Still, something told her that while this man might do everything in his power to get into her drawers, and every other woman's, he would never use force. Part of the thrill for a man like Cutter would be the sheer act of seduction itself, the verbal and emotional foreplay. And Cutter Beaumont seemed to know just how to go about it. She was going to have to proceed with caution.

"I'm not running from anything, Mr. Beaumont," she said, trying to come up with a way to discourage him. "Just because I don't get a major thrill out of sitting in some man's mobile home watching his coon dogs scratch their undersides—"

She hoped she hadn't gone too far. He looked genuinely offended. All the light went out of his eyes. Finally, he shoved his hat back on his head and jerked the door open. "I'll get your bags," he said, making his way across the front porch and out the door without another word. Ellie followed and held the door open for him. She had made him mad. She could see it in the tensing of his jaw, the way he carried her bags in and dumped them unceremoniously in the front room. The cardboard box holding her books landed on the floor with a thud. "If that's all, I'll be going now," he said, his face as hard as granite. "My deputy will be making rounds later. Be sure to let him know if you need anything."

Ellie could see that he was clearly peeved. She realized he *had* gone to a lot of trouble for her. Maybe she had been too rough on him. Lord knew she was out of practice where the opposite sex was concerned. While she desperately wanted to keep him at arm's length, she certainly didn't want to make an enemy out of him. "Before you go, Sheriff—" She reached into her purse, pulled out a crisp ten dollar bill, and held it out to him. "Why don't you go buy yourself a couple of six packs?" She smiled warmly at him, hoping to make amends.

The scowl on Cutter's face told her she had not made the right decision by offering to pay him. "I'm not a bellboy, lady," he said, "and I don't accept tips." He started out the door, then paused. "Actually, I was just trying to be neighborly, but that's obviously not something you're used to, coming from the big city and all. When you get that bur out of your behind, you may want to make a few friends on this island. Let me know when you're ready."

With that he was gone, leaving Ellie to feel more than a little silly for having overreacted in the first place. What was wrong with her, anyway? But she already knew. Cutter Beaumont was the first man in more than a year to attract her interest.

And that frightened her.

Three

Ellie stood at the front door for a long time after Cutter's Jeep disappeared, wishing she had not reacted so negatively. It was her fault, she knew, because she spent so much time second-guessing everything people said and did. Why did she invest so much energy in looking for ulterior motives? Well, she *knew* why, she reminded herself. She simply had no idea how to change it.

Finally, Ellie carried her luggage into the back bedroom, having already decided that was where she would be most comfortable. The old four-poster bed with its faded quilt was as inviting as a warm kitchen on a winter's day. She set her suitcases on the bed, unlocked them, and flipped open the latches. Since she didn't plan to dress up much while on the island, she had packed only one nice outfit, as well as a couple of simple cotton dresses. She shook them out and hung them in the back of the closet, then concentrated on unpacking the items she *planned* to wear: jeans and shorts and T-shirts. After six years of business suits and high heels, she looked forward to knocking around in something comfortable.

Ellie wondered if she would miss her job at the hotel, and the thought that she probably wouldn't made her sad. Until a year earlier her career had meant everything. She had worked her way up from convention and catering manager to assistant manager and finally the coveted position of general manager for one of the most prestigious hotels in Savannah. And then suddenly it hadn't mattered anymore. Not her job or the luxury condo she'd sunk her savings into or the interesting friends she'd made over the years. Nothing had mattered anymore. She'd felt dead inside.

Ellie sometimes feared she was losing her mind.

"You have *obviously* lost your mind," her mother had said weeks before, when Ellie had told her she'd leased a house on Erskine. "You can't just quit your job and move to a deserted island where they don't even have a beauty parlor." Nelda Parks epitomized the true Southern belle of old. Her manners were as perfect as her linen suits and blue-gray hairdo. She was as dainty and graceful as a spring butterfly without losing one ounce of dignity.

"I'm not quitting my job, Mother. I'm taking a leave of absence. And it's not a deserted island. There are plenty of people there. At least fifty or sixty. And did I tell you Erskine is completely crime free?"

This didn't seem to appease the woman in the least. "Have you talked this over with that nice little doctor friend of yours, dear?"

Her mother sometimes got on Ellie's nerves. Not only was she a hypochondriac and a worrywart who seldom stopped talking long enough to listen, she could be self-centered and a bit of a snob too. Luckily she had a few redeeming traits that made her faults more tolerable, but Ellie couldn't think of what they were at the moment.

Ellie was nothing like her mother. Born into the world weighing a robust nine pounds, she had learned from the beginning she was going to have to be tough to survive in a household with three brothers. Nelda Parks didn't try to hide her disappointment when her only daughter turned into a tomboy at an early age and spent most of her waking hours atop some tree. Ellie was the first girl in the neighborhood to play Little League ball, and she could beat all the boys in her fifth grade class in arm wrestling. It came as no surprise that she excelled in sports, winning medals in track and swimming. She grew into a lovely, self-confident woman who was not afraid of anything.

But all that had changed one night in a dark parking lot.

Ellie realized her mother was watching her curiously, waiting for some sort of reply. "Dr. Brenner is not my nice little doctor friend, Mother. She's a licensed psychologist. A shrink, as Daddy would call her," she added. "And no, I haven't discussed this with her. As a matter of fact, I've stopped seeing her altogether."

"This is going to absolutely kill your father, you know," her mother whispered. "It's bad enough we had to suffer all that nasty business last year . . . the hospital and the police. I just hope you can live with yourself when your father is dead of a heart attack."

Ellie was tired of hearing how sick her father was when she knew there wasn't a damn thing wrong with him, tired of hearing how her attack the year before had hurt her family. *What about me*, she wanted to say. *She* had suffered. *She* had changed and would never again be the person she once was. But Ellie hadn't said those things, because she knew they would only upset her mother further. "Daddy already knows about Erskine," she said instead, "and he thinks it's a great idea."

"Why am I always the last to know anything that happens in this family?" Nelda complained.

"Because you don't make it easy, Mother," Ellie had told her, and the other woman had sulked and picked at her lunch afterward like a recalcitrant child.

Now, as Ellie unpacked the rest of her clothes, she wished she had been kinder to the woman. She decided, as she stuck her suitcases into a closet for storage, that she would make it up to her by writing long, newsy letters while she was away. She would learn to be more tolerant. After all, she had not been so easy to get along with this past year either.

Ellie went into the kitchen to search for something to cut the twine off the cardboard box containing books and suddenly found herself staring into a drawer of butcher knives. Her facial muscles froze into a grim expression as she selected the least deadly looking one from the group. She studied it, turning the blade this way and that. It caught the light and flashed once, and she was reminded of another flash of blade, another time, when she had learned to fear dark parking lots and just about everything else in life. She continued to stare at the knife, mesmerized by the smooth handle in her closed palm. She ran her index finger along the blunt side of the blade and found it cool to her touch. Cold steel. She was as fascinated with it as she was terrified.

Very carefully, Ellie carried the knife into the next room. She didn't draw a breath of relief until she had finished using it and stuck it back in the drawer out of sight. But her hands trembled nevertheless as she unpacked the box.

Ellie discovered a small black-and-white portable television set in another bedroom closet when she checked to see if there was space for her books. She carried it into the kitchen, set it on the counter, and plugged it in, hoping it would work. Surprisingly enough it did, although the reception was a bit snowy. She suspected the TV would be her only link to civilization while she was on Erskine. Not that she had cared much what was going on in the outside world lately, she realized. There had been so much going on *inside* of her that she'd had little time for anything else.

Ellie flipped the channel, wondering what she would find playing this time of day. With the demands of her job at the hotel she'd never had much time for television or reading or the dozen or so other things she'd wanted to do. Over the next few weeks she planned to make up for that fact. She would stay up late and sleep till noon. She would read everything she could get her hands on, starting with her box of paperbacks. She would go without makeup and walk around in her bare feet like she had as a child. She would lie in the sun and fish and maybe, if she had time left over, she would teach herself how to cook. She almost groaned aloud at the thought of trying to improve her culinary skills. It had occurred to her once or twice that she would have to eat her own cooking while she was on Erskine, where there were no fast-food restaurants. She only hoped Cutter carried frozen dinners in his store.

Ellie continued to change the channels, adjusting the antenna so she could get a better picture. Once it cleared, she found herself looking into the faces of a beautifully dressed man and woman who were locked in a heated embrace. The man seemed consumed with the woman in his arms, kissing her face and eyelids. Their passion was almost palpable, drawing Ellie in closer and closer so that she felt as if she had somehow stepped into the scene. She closed her eyes and brushed her fingers across her bottom lip and tried to remember the last time a man had kissed her in a romantic sort of way. Suddenly, she thought of Cutter; the pitch-colored eyes, those full lips, that darkly sensual face. She wondered what it would be like to kiss him or be kissed by him and her face warmed at the mental image of Cutter coaxing her mouth open with his tongue, of Cutter slipping his hands beneath her blouse, cupping one breast in a callused palm. She shivered; more in delight than fear.

Cutter muttered a whole string of obscenities when he arrived back at the saloon and discovered Ellie's checkbook had somehow fallen out of her purse onto the floor of the Jeep. He had the urge to throw the damn thing in the water and keep going. It would serve her right, he told himself.

He climbed back into his Jeep. He'd take the damn thing back to her, because if he didn't, she'd just come looking for it. He didn't need any more grief, especially from some skinny, pale-faced city woman who thought she was too good for the likes of him.

Cutter drove back to the Simmses' place, parked, and hurried to the house, deciding he had wasted enough time for one day. Crossing the front porch, he saw the door was ajar. He tapped once, and it swung open. For a moment he considered leaving the checkbook just inside the door, but the sound of voices coming from the back of the house made him curious. He pushed the door open further and walked in.

She was standing in the kitchen, her eyes glued to a small TV set. Cutter followed her gaze and grinned when he saw what she was watching. Interesting stuff, he thought. But not half as interesting as the look on Ellie Parks's face.

Something stirred low in his belly as he watched her watching the couple on the screen. He wondered if the rest of her body was responding as well. His certainly was. Not from the program, but from the look on her face. He could feel the pressure building behind his zipper. If he didn't do something fast, he was going to end up embarrassing himself.

"You're going to turn into a sex maniac if you watch too much of that stuff," he said.

His voice, breaking into Ellie's dulled senses, had the effect of a stick of dynamite going off in the room. She whirled around and screamed loud enough to shatter glass.

Cutter stood perfectly still as he watched the sweet young thing before him transform into something from a Bruce Lee film. Her bared nails looked as ominous as lawn-mower blades, and the look in her eyes told him she wouldn't think twice before removing that part of his person responsible for childbearing. And then recognition hit, and her fear was replaced by anger.

"What the hell are you doing here?" Ellie demanded, not altering her stance whatsoever.

"I brought you this." He indicated the checkbook with a nod. "I got all the way back to the saloon before I noticed it. Must've fallen out of your purse."

She cut off the rest of his explanation. "Why didn't you knock?"

Cutter regretted now that he hadn't thrown the thing in the water after all. "I *did* knock. But you were obviously so involved in your program, you didn't hear me." He motioned toward the television set where the couple was still engaged in what was turning out to be a marathon kissing event.

Ellie's face flamed. He was making fun of her. "You have no right to walk in uninvited."

Cutter set the checkbook on the table and regarded her, hands on hips, head cocked insolently to one side. "Tell me something, Miz Parks," he said. "Are you mad 'cause I came in without your permission, or are you just embarrassed 'cause I caught you all hot and bothered over some couple smooching?"

Embarrassed wasn't the word. She was mortified. "Please leave."

"Gladly." He started for the door, then paused. "By the way. If I were you, I'd pay close attention to those love scenes. With your disposition, that's as close as you're going to come to the real thing." He was gone before she could respond. Ellie locked the door behind him.

"That should keep him out," she muttered under her breath.

That's as close as you're going to come to the real thing.

She was surprised how much his statement hurt her feelings.

Ellie spent the next hour dusting and cleaning with a vengeance, deciding that she wasn't about to let Cutter Beaumont ruin her first day on Erskine. She'd had a major purpose for coming: rest and relaxation and maybe, if she was lucky, a little peace of mind and some old-fashioned healing. Nobody, not even that cocky, swaggering sheriff and saloon owner was going to take that away from her. Finally, after clearing away the dust and cobwebs, Ellie decided she deserved a break.

She let herself out the back door a moment later, pausing on the steps as she took in the yard that resembled a jungle with its palmetto fans and cypress and wild ferns. The smell of honeysuckle sweetened the air, mingling with the salty breeze off the ocean, which was blocked from view by a strip of forest. Nevertheless, Ellie could make out the faint sound of waves crashing on the beach. She planned to visit it later. Here and there she heard a dog bark and wondered if any of them belonged to Cutter. She wondered once more why he got under her skin so. There was just something about the man, the way he looked at her, that smile that made her feel as if he knew what color panties she had on.

Ellie spied the garden spot along the edge of the yard where the trees thinned enough to let the sun through. Someone had obviously gone to a lot of trouble to have good topsoil brought in, because the dirt there was rich and black, unlike the sand-and-clay mixture that made up much of the island. Twelve-foot sections of railroad ties surrounded it and held it in place. Ellie knelt beside the garden, scooped up a handful of the soil, and raised it to her nose. It was warm and fragrant. She smiled at the simple pleasure it brought her, and for a moment she remained perfectly still, enjoying the sun on her face and the peaceful feelings inside. Perhaps this was what healing was all about, she thought. Ellie continued to kneel there, quietly reflecting, until a small noise intruded on her thoughts. She turned to see a young woman and child veer off the dirt road and come toward her. Ellie recognized Franklin D. immediately.

"Miss Simms's son brung that dirt over from the mainland," the woman said without preamble when she stepped closer. "You thinkin' of havin' a garden?"

Ellie dusted off her hands and stood. "I don't know much about gardening, I'm afraid."

"Ain't nothin' to it. I could show you. My name's Rose Wilcox. I think you done met my son Franklin D."

Ellie smiled at the woman, then turned her attention to the boy. "Yes, we met when I first arrived. Franklin D. watched my bags for me."

"Then you'd be the one who gave him this dollar bill?" Rose said, indicating the money in her son's tightly clenched fist.

Ellie remembered how insulted Cutter had been when she'd tried to pay him, and she hoped she hadn't managed to offend the boy's mother as well. "I didn't mean any harm," she said. "Franklin D. earned that money."

Rose looked relieved to hear it. "Oh, I don't mind you payin' him for doin' you a service. I just wanted to make sure he didn't take something that didn't belong to him," she said. "I've had to take a hickory switch to him once or twice for stealin'."

Ellie was glad she'd been able to save the boy from such an ordeal. She smiled at him. "Actually, I was hoping Franklin D. would buy himself a comic book with the money."

Rose laughed and Ellie noted the woman was very pretty when she smiled. "Lordy, this boy already has a whole room full of 'em." She patted her son on the head and gazed down at him through loving black eyes. "But I reckon one more won't hurt. Okay, son, you can keep the money. Seein' how you earned it fair and square." She returned her attention to Ellie. "So you're the lady from Savannah. I heard you was pretty." She chuckled at the look of surprise on Ellie's face. "Word travels fast on this island."

"My name is Ellie Parks," she said, reaching out to shake hands with the woman. "Have you lived on Erskine long?" Ellie asked.

The young woman nodded. "All my life. My husband and I were both raised here. I reckon we'll die here too." She studied Ellie closely. "So what made you come to Erskine?"

"I'm sort of on vacation," Ellie told her. "I wanted to find a place with peace and quiet."

Rose laughed. "Then you shoulda never moved next door to Cutter Beaumont and his dogs."

"Are they noisy?"

"Only when they get riled. But it's not too bad considering how he looks out for everybody. Miz Simms woulda never been able to stay alone as long as she did if it hadn't been for Cutter looking after her. Which is why we don't much mind when he gets a wild hair once in a while. Me and my family live on the other side of Cutter. You need somethin', you come to me." She said it matter-of-factly. "I got me another boy at home. His name is Booker T., and he's ten."

"The deputy told me you named your children after important people."

The woman nodded. "I lost one son a couple of years ago in an accident. Named him George Washington Carver Wilcox, after a great black scientist. My husband says it's silly to name our boys after great men, but I don't care. I want more for my boys than my folks wanted for me."

Ellie decided she liked Rose Wilcox. "Listen, all I have to offer you is cold water at the moment, but you're welcome to come in out of the sun for a while." She indicated the house.

"I can't stay," Rose told her. "My husband'll be home from work soon. He's a shrimper who likes his dinner on the table when he comes in the front door." She turned to go, then paused. "You be sure to visit, y'hear? Most of these folks don't take to new faces, but I ain't like that."

"Thanks. I might just do that." Ellie watched the two take to the dirt road once again, moving slowly under the afternoon sun as though they had all day to get where they were going. They disappeared a moment later around a bend. Ellie glanced at her watch and realized it was after two o'clock and she hadn't had lunch. As if acting on cue, her stomach growled. She decided she had better get a move on and go to the grocery store if she expected to eat.

Ellie quickly ran a brush through her hair, grabbed her wallet and keys, and headed toward town. Or what there was of a town, she thought.

Here and there, she caught glimpses of the surrounding ocean, and she couldn't wait to test it out later.

Ellie passed a couple of people on the way to the store, an elderly man on a bicycle, then a uniformed man driving a moped with the words U.S. MAIL stenciled on leather pouches hanging from the back. She smiled and waved, and the man nodded curtly and continued chugging down the road. So, the islanders weren't crazy about having outsiders around, she thought.

Once Ellie reached the clearing of trees that made up the town of Erskine, she paused and glanced around at the activity. A group of women chatted beneath one of the tall live oaks as the ferryboat, the same one she'd come over on earlier, docked and let off a dozen or more schoolchildren. Ellie smiled as the students hurried toward their mothers. She was still smiling as she made her way up the front porch to the store, where two elderly men sat on a wooden bench and watched passersby. From somewhere she caught the faint sounds of a country music song and decided it must be coming from the saloon. As she made her way up to the door of the store she noticed the Closed sign. Thinking it must be a mistake, she tried the knob and found it locked.

"Store's closed," one of the men said.

Ellie turned toward them. "I thought it stayed open in the evenings until nine o'clock."

One of the men looked up and spat something black into the dirt, then wiped his mouth. "Sheriff closed it early today," he said.

"Oh?" Ellie said, wondering why Cutter hadn't bothered to tell her he was going to close the store early, when he knew she needed groceries. Her stomach growled again. "Do you know where I can find the sheriff?"

The men offered her a blank stare. "Where you can always find him," one of them said. "In the saloon."

Wearing a frown of irritation, Ellie crossed the front porch to the door leading inside the saloon. She opened it, stepped inside, and waited for her eyes to adjust to the dim light. Her mouth watered when she smelled chili cooking, as well as onion rings. It didn't take long for her to spot Cutter standing behind the bar.

"I need to talk to you," she said.

He glanced up quickly at the sound of her voice. "What's your problem *now*, lady?"

"You closed the store."

"Yeah, so?"

She crossed her arms. "You knew darn good and well I needed to buy food today." When he merely shrugged, she went on. "Are you so hard up for a dinner date that you have to stoop to something like this?" She regretted it the moment she said it. It sounded silly and childish but, darn it all, she was hot and tired and half-starved.

Cutter stopped what he was doing and stared at her. "What are you talking about?

She had no choice but to explain herself. "The fact that I chose not to have dinner with you," she said. "Is this your way of getting even with me?" Even as she said it, Ellie realized her timing wasn't the greatest. She had drawn the attention of every man in the room. For a moment she almost felt bad for Cutter. Now everybody on the island would know she had rejected his overtures. Well, that's just tough, she thought. Cutter Beaumont deserved every bit of it, if this was the way he did business.

Cutter stepped from behind the bar, his black eyes fastened on hers. "No, that's not why I closed the store," he said softly. "The lady who runs it got sick today and had to leave early. But if you need something, all you have to do is tell me and I'll open it for you."

His voice would have coaxed the hide off a bear. Ellie suddenly felt very foolish. She glanced around and found every eye in the place on her. A rosy blush stained her cheeks as she turned her attention back to Cutter. "I didn't know," she said lamely.

"Of course not. But that didn't stop you from stomping in here and accusing me of all sorts of things, did it?" He didn't give her a chance to respond. "You need something out of the store, Ellie, just say so."

She wanted to crawl into a hole and die. "You said you were closed."

"So I've reopened." Cutter motioned to a tall man watching the big-screen TV. "Bart, can you keep an eye on things in here while I run next door?" The man nodded and made his way toward the bar.

Cutter walked to the door that led to his store, opened it, and switched on a light. He motioned for Ellie to pass through first. "You'll find baskets over there," he told her. "Get what you need and I'll check you out." He took a seat on the stool behind the cash register and waited.

"I'll just pick up a few things," Ellie said, feeling guilty for all she'd said to him, especially in front of his customers. What was wrong with her? Why did she insist on taking everything he said or did the wrong way? Because you're attracted to him, she told herself, and you know you've no right to be. And because you don't have the first clue how to act in front of a man anymore.

"Take your time," Cutter said, leafing through a magazine as though he had nothing better to do. He was as laid-back as the rest of the islanders in that respect.

Retrieving a basket from the front of the store, Ellie slipped the cloth handle over her arm and made for the dairy case, where she selected milk, eggs, butter, cheese, and a variety of packaged meats. Once she had loaded up on the necessities, she raided the potato chip and candy aisle, knowing it was a bad idea to shop for food when she was so hungry.

"You know this stuff's bad for you," Cutter told her as he rang them up.

Ellie smiled at him. "I suppose I owe you an apology."

He paused and looked at her. "Lady, you don't owe me a damn thing."

"I'm sorry," she said, nevertheless. "I shouldn't have jumped all over you the way I did. Especially in front of your customers." He continued what he was doing as though he hadn't heard her. "I'd like to make it up to you."

This time he completely stopped what he was doing. "What'd you have in mind?"

"Well . . ." she hesitated. She had been rude and thoughtless toward him when all he'd done since she'd arrived was try to be neighborly. "Is that invitation to dinner still open?" she asked.

Cutter tried not to show his pleasure. It wouldn't do for him to get cocky or arrogant now, *now*, after he'd plotted so carefully to get what he wanted. He could see the shame in her eyes, see that she was willing to do just about anything to make up to him for yelling at him in front of his customers. He really was a low-down skunk to have closed the store down just so she'd have to come crawling to him, but a man had to do what a man had to do.

"Yeah, dinner's still open," he said after a moment. "You bring the dessert."

She held up the box of chocolate-covered donuts she'd just bought. "No problem."

Four

Once Ellie carried her sack of groceries home and unloaded them, she changed into a pair of shorts and an old sweatshirt and made her way through the forest behind her house to the beach on the other side. Although she knew she couldn't stay long, she at least had to see it.

To say that the view was breathtaking was simply not enough. Ellie stood there, momentarily dazed, as she took it all in. It was like nothing she had ever seen. And she had seen her share of ritzy beaches in her travels on hotel business.

Ellie tested the water with one toe and found it surprisingly warm, even though summer was still almost three months away. She walked farther out, until the water slapped at her calves. She closed her eyes and inhaled the salt-kissed breeze, let it play through her hair while her toes sank into the soft sand. The late-afternoon sun felt wonderful on her face. She smiled and gave in to the relaxing sensations, waves crashing against the shore, the cry of seagulls.

This is what she had come for, she told herself. The peace and serenity. She could almost feel the healing taking place inside her. But even more surprising, astonishing actually, she wasn't dreading the fact she was going to have to spend a portion of her evening with Cutter Beaumont. In a way, she was looking forward to it. She trusted him for reasons she wasn't quite sure of, and that *had* to be a good sign that she was getting better.

Ellie walked a distance, then reluctantly turned back so she would have time to shower and change before going to Cutter's place. Several times her insecurities flared up and she thought of cancelling, then reminded herself the Simmses' phones had long ago been disconnected. Although her mother had been horrified at the thought of having no way to contact her, Ellie liked the idea and hadn't bothered to have the phones hooked up for the period of time she planned to be there. She could call anyone *she* wanted to, whenever *she* wanted to, from the pay phone at the store. But if she wanted to take the coward's way out and cancel her dinner with Cutter, she would have to walk over there personally and do it. She would simply have to put her fears aside and go. It would be a learning experience. She *needed* to learn how to deal with the opposite sex again, if only on a *strictly friends* basis. It was time she made positive steps in the right direction. Every time she took one step forward in putting her life back together, it boosted her ego and made tackling the next step just a bit easier. Perhaps complete recovery was only a few steps away. She wanted to return to Savannah the same Ellie she'd been before her attack.

Back at the house Ellie took a quick shower,

slipped on a pair of jeans, a cotton sweater, and old sneakers. She combed her wet hair straight back, deciding to let it dry naturally, and she didn't even bother with makeup. The last thing she wanted to do was look like she was dressing up for a date. Lord knew, Cutter Beaumont didn't need prompting. Finally, she stacked the chocolate-covered donuts on a plate and set out for Cutter's place.

Ellie wasn't sure what she'd been expecting before she spied his neat log cabin–looking structure in the woods, but one would never have guessed it was a double-wide mobile home from the outside. At the bottom, where the wheels would have been, someone had obviously spent a good deal of time and money framing it in with stone. There was even a front porch complete with two old-fashioned wicker rockers. Off to one side were various outbuildings and a large pen for his dogs. As though sensing her presence, several of the hounds started to bark. By the time Ellie reached Cutter's porch, they were yapping and howling and doing their level best to climb the tall pen. Suddenly the front door of the trailer was thrown open and Cutter was yelling at the top of his lungs for them to shut up.

Ellie almost dropped her plate of donuts at the sight of him barefoot and bare chested in a pair of shamefully tight jeans. She opened her mouth to speak but nothing came out. Cutter grinned. "It's okay," he said, as though he thought her sudden attack of nerves was due to his dogs. "I know they sound vicious, but they're really harmless. Unless you smell like coon, which you don't."

Ellie paused halfway across the porch. "Am I early?" she asked, trying to keep her gaze fixed on his face and pretend she wasn't the least bit interested in that massive chest or the thick black mat of hair covering it.

As if realizing he was half-naked, Cutter glanced at himself, then back at her. "No, *I'm* late. The guy who sometimes runs the saloon for me at night was late coming in. I just climbed out of the shower." He stepped aside and held the door open wider. "Come on in."

Ellie didn't like it one bit. It was bad enough she was having dinner at some stranger's house in the middle of the woods. Under any other circumstances she wouldn't have even considered such a thing. She tried to remind herself she was dealing with an island authority, a man of the law. Rose Wilcox had said good things about this man. Still, every instinct in her body told her to proceed with caution. "Maybe I should just wait out here until you finish getting ready," she said.

"Don't be silly. It'll only take me a minute."

Reluctantly, Ellie stepped through the front door. Cutter closed it, and the sound startled her so badly, she jumped. Had she put herself in a dangerous situation? she wondered. Had she allowed herself to be charmed into trusting him by that good-ol-boy routine of his, only to be lured into his home, where she was at a disadvantage? Just looking at him, his wide chest and shoulders, she knew she was no match.

"Would you like a cold beer?" Cutter asked, going to the refrigerator and opening it. When she merely nodded, he pulled out two bottles and twisted off the tops. "Here, have a seat," he said, indicating the counter where two barstools rested. "Let me grab a shirt."

Ellie didn't draw a sigh of relief until he was

gone. She set her beer bottle on the counter and stood beside the front door for a moment, torn between staying and running as far away from Cutter Beaumont as she could get. All her old fears reared their ugly heads.

"What's wrong, Ellie?" he said when he returned, fastening the buttons on his shirt. He could tell she was uncomfortable. Scared, actually.

Ellie suddenly felt trapped, all alone with him, the door closed, blocking her passage. It was insane, but it was happening just the same, and there wasn't a damn thing she could do about it. She reached for the knob with trembling fingers. "I was just going to have a look at your dogs," she said. "Do you mind?"

He looked surprised. "I wouldn't have figured you for a lover of coon dogs. I'll go with you." He grabbed their beers and joined her on the porch, where he handed her one of the bottles. Watching her curiously, he followed her out to the pen and introduced her to his prize bluetick hounds. "I'm actually more interested in breeding these dogs than making hunters out of them. They've put out some good stock. 'Course, I take them out every now and then just to make sure they can still tree a coon. And to let them get some exercise." Cutter realized she wasn't listening to a word he was saying.

"Ellie?"

Ellie glanced up at him and found him watching her, a thoughtful expression in his eyes. "Yes?"

"I've never physically hurt a woman in my life."

"So?"

"So you can stop looking at me as though you think I might."

She laughed self-consciously and turned away. "I'm sorry, I didn't realize I was."

He took a swig of his beer and leaned against one of the posts securing the pen. "Want to talk about it?"

"What?"

"Whatever's bothering you."

"No."

"Might help."

"I doubt it."

"Look, Ellie, I believe everybody is entitled to a little bit of privacy, myself included, but I hate to see someone so . . ." He paused and studied the look on her face.

"Uptight?"

He shrugged. "Yeah."

"I've always been a rather private sort of person, I suppose," she said at last. "I'm not that comfortable around people."

"How could you manage a big, fancy hotel and not like people?"

"How do you know what I do for a living?" she asked, suddenly alarmed that he knew so much about her. It made her wonder what else he knew.

"Relax, it was in the lease agreement you signed. Mrs. Simms's son mailed me a copy of it."

"Oh."

"So, what's the story, Ellie Parks? What made you decide to run away from an uptown place like Savannah and hide out on Erskine?"

Ellie took a sip of her beer and tried not to wrinkle her face in distaste. She had never been a beer drinker, but then, she had never lived on a remote island either. "What makes you think I'm hiding?"

He glanced around. "This isn't exactly a booming metropolis, you know. I can't imagine a pretty young thing like you wanting to come here. If you *are* hiding from something, I'd like to know."

She studied him for a moment. "Why?"

"Well, I *am* the sheriff. I think I have the right to know what you're doing here."

"So you're asking out of professional curiosity?"

He smiled. "Not entirely. But that's a good place to start."

"Don't worry, I haven't committed any sort of crime. As a matter of fact, I've never even had so much as a parking ticket."

"Then it's not so much *what* you're hiding from but *who*? Is it a man?" The telltale blush on her face told him he was getting warm, and it irked the hell out of him to think she might be involved with someone. "What'd he do?" When she didn't respond, he went on. "Let me guess. You caught your old man in the sack with another woman."

"No. It's nothing like that." Ellie wished it were that simple. She could get over something like that.

"So what is it?"

She forced herself to meet his gaze. "I was attacked last year," she said, willing herself to remain matter-of-fact about it. "A man accosted me in a dark parking lot as I was leaving work." Ellie wasn't sure when the changes in Cutter took place. One moment he was smiling, that teasing light in his dark eyes, the next minute all the light was gone.

"He raped you?"

Finally, she looked away. "I don't wish to go into the details, but, yes, he did rape me."

"Did they catch him?"

"No. The police are still looking. Every now and

then they call me in to look at a lineup, but nothing so far." She sighed and met his gaze once again. "So now you see why I'm a little anxious . . . around men."

"You haven't been with a man since?"

Under any other circumstances she would have thought the question much too personal. At the moment, though, it seemed only natural he should ask her. "No, I haven't. I've avoided relationships altogether. Now, could we talk about something else? The only reason I told you this was so you'd understand why I'm like I am."

The tense lines around her eyes and mouth told Cutter it had been excruciatingly hard for her to talk about it. He wanted to tell her he was sorry it had happened, but he was half afraid she would burst into tears and that was one thing he couldn't handle. "So what you're telling me is we probably won't have sex tonight," he said instead.

At first she was shocked. Then, when she realized he was merely trying to lessen the tension between them, Ellie chuckled. "Or any other night."

He raised the beer bottle to his lips once again. "Never say never, Ellie. I might be just the cure you're looking for." When she started to object, he raised a finger and planted it against her lips. "But rest assured, when it happens, you're going to want it just as much as I do."

"You've got one helluva ego, Cutter Beaumont," she said, laughing up at him. Suddenly she felt safe again. He might be a rogue and a scoundrel, but her instincts told her he would never use physical force. Male pride alone wouldn't let him. *Lord, let my instincts be right,* she thought.

He winked. "And when you get to know me better, you'll understand why I have this enormous ego." The teasing light was back in his eyes. He was determined to see that she relaxed and had a good time. "You ready to eat? I'm starved." He grinned. "Or would you rather eat out here, where you can break into a fast run if I lose control all of a sudden?"

She laughed. "No, I'm okay now." And she was. It hadn't been easy telling him, but now she was glad she had. And she knew, without having to ask him, that he would keep the information confidential.

Cutter led her back to the house, where he finished putting dinner together while Ellie watched from her seat at the counter. "I like your place," she said, glancing around the living room. Although it was tasteful and neat, it was still a man's place, with its leather furniture and earth-tone colors. There were no lace doilies or baskets of dried flowers, anything to suggest a woman's touch in planning the decor. "It's nice."

Cutter glanced up at her from the counter. "You sound surprised. What were you expecting it to look like? Graceland?" The guilty look on her face told him he was right on target. "I have a Lava lamp in my bedroom," he said. "My only tribute to the late sixties. You can see that next time."

She had to smile at that. "I won't be going into your bedroom, Sheriff."

He shrugged, but he didn't look convinced. "Whatever you say." He went back to work. Once he'd filled two bowls with rice and gumbo and cut thick slices of French bread and put them on a plate, he pronounced dinner served. "What do you think?" he asked when she had tasted a mouthful.

Ellie nodded enthusiastically. "It's great."

"Not too spicy?"

"No, I love hot stuff."

"So do I." She blushed, and he knew he'd gotten his point across.

When they finished dinner, Ellie offered to clean up and Cutter was only too happy to oblige as he helped himself to a chocolate donut. "I hope you won't think I'm a party pooper if I leave early," she told him once she'd loaded the dishes into the dishwasher and wiped the counters clean. "I'm really tired."

"You could always spend the night here."

"Very funny."

"Okay, I'll walk you back. I have to run by the saloon anyway and make sure everything's okay." He grabbed a flashlight from the top of his refrigerator.

"You don't have to walk me back," she said, not wanting him to think she was anxious about cutting through the wooded area in the dark.

He shrugged and made his way to the door, then switched on the light to make sure it worked. "I don't mind. It's the least I can do after that fine dessert you brought. Besides, we've got snakes out here as long as my legs."

Ellie came to a screeching halt. "You do?"

"Yeah, but I'll protect you." When she didn't so much as budge, he grinned. "It's okay, they're scared of the light. But if you get bit, I'll personally suck all the poison out."

That was the problem with the man, Ellie decided as she followed him out the door and across the front porch. One could never know for sure whether he was serious or not. "You'd do that for me?" she asked, determined not to let on how nervous she was over the possibility of something slithering across her foot. Of course he wouldn't have to suck out the poison, because just the sight of a snake would send her into cardiac arrest and she'd be dead before she hit the ground. "Be careful or I'm going to mistake you for a gentleman," she said with a lightness she didn't feel.

Cutter chuckled. "That would be the biggest mistake of your life," he said. "I've never pretended to be a gentleman, not even when it was in my own best interest to do so."

Ellie glanced at him. She could barely make out his profile in the moonlight. "Oh? When was that?"

He waved off the remark. "A long time ago. In another life."

Ellie got the impression he didn't wish to elaborate. Probably had something to do with his ex-wife. But she didn't push. After all, he had not demanded to know more about her attack even though he'd been clearly curious. She appreciated that, and it made her even more respectful of his privacy. At the same time, she got the impression there was more to this man than met the eye. Much more.

"Well, thanks for dinner," she said once they'd reached her yard. She offered her hand.

Cutter held it tightly. "Aren't you going to invite me in for a nightcap?"

He looked so surprised that she hadn't asked him, it was almost funny. "No, I'm not." She pulled her hand free.

"Another time then." He said it as if he were willing to bet his next paycheck on it.

Ellie shook her head, a smile teasing the corners of her lips. The man was about as cocky as they came. And with good reason, she thought, gazing at his darkly handsome face. She was certain there were other women on the island who would be only too happy to invite him in. "I doubt it, Sheriff."

Her voice had a lilting, melodious sound to it that warmed his belly like good brandy, then went straight to his head. But it was those lips that were his undoing. Cutter knew he was going to kiss her come hell or high water, and his ego told him she probably wouldn't mind. When it came to moonlight and soft breezes, most women were suckers for romance. Ellie Parks, even with her traumatic past, would be no different. He stepped closer, saw her look of surprise, then captured her mouth before she could say anything. To say that she was shocked would have been an understatement; he could feel the automatic stiffening of her body. He understood. It made him even more determined to move slowly and handle her with a lot of TLC. But the moment he slipped his arms around her waist and pulled her against him, his body snapped alive. She was softer than anything he'd ever known, and her body fit perfectly against his. He explored the small of her back, her round hips, and thought he had surely died and gone to paradise. Eagerly, he prodded her lips apart with his tongue. She tried to speak but the sound was muffled.

Ellie felt the panic rise in the back of her throat the moment Cutter's mouth found hers. She tried to object but when she opened her mouth, he speared his tongue deeply inside. She pushed with all her might, but she may as well have been trying to move a mountain. Finally, she wrenched her mouth free. "Don't," she said, craning her neck so that he couldn't find her lips. She could feel his breath at her ear. But that wasn't the scary part. The scary part was feeling his hardness against her belly and not knowing whether he planned to use it on her or not. Had she made a mistake by trusting him? Had he purposely set out to earn her confidence, only to take advantage of her later?

Cutter couldn't think past the taste and feel of her. He dropped the flashlight and they were cloaked in darkness. "You're making this more complicated than it has to be," he whispered. "I could help you overcome your problem. You don't have to be afraid anymore. We would be good together, Ellie." She was shaking her head so fast it was impossible to see her face. He captured her head between his palms. The look she gave him had the same effect on him a handful of ice thrust down the front of his jeans would have had. She was frightened. Terrified, actually. That hadn't been his intent. "Ellie?" He shook her slightly.

She started to tremble. She had trusted this man. She had told him the truth about herself, had sat beside him at dinner, had thought they might be friends. Now she was standing in the dark with him and he was free to do with her whatever he wished. "Let me go," she demanded between clenched teeth.

Cutter released her so fast, he almost sent her toppling backward. "Okay," he said. He backed away, both hands held high in surrender. "You're free to go."

Once she had gotten past her fear, Ellie was mad enough to spit. "How could you?"

He felt like a heel. "Look, Ellie, I'm sorry. You

can't blame a guy for trying. I had no idea it was this bad for you. I just thought—"

"You thought what?" she demanded. "That your expert lovemaking would cure my fears?"

"I've heard of worse ideas."

"I don't believe you! I go through crisis counseling and therapy and everything I can think of, and nothing works. But Cutter Beaumont, island stud, is going to fix me like new with his incredible lovemaking."

She was making fun of him, and Cutter didn't like it one bit. "Look, I said I was sorry."

"Just stay away from me," she said, a sob catching in the back of her throat. She turned and ran for the house.

Nobody had warned her about the mosquitoes. Ellie felt something light on her arm and slapped it, but she wasn't quick enough and it got away. The pesky insect would be back and add more welts on the growing number already present on her bare arms and legs. But she was too mad to care at the moment. Dressed in a pair of shorty pajamas, she sat on the metal glider on the front porch and stewed over what Cutter Beaumont had said only an hour before.

You're making this more complicated than it has to be. I could help you overcome your problem. You don't have to be afraid anymore.

Ellie's eyes burned with tears. What did Cutter Beaumont know? He had never suffered the humiliation of rape. He'd never had to beg for his life. He'd never felt a knife pierce his flesh or watched his own blood pool around his feet.

Ellie closed her eyes tightly, wanting to stop the

images that filled her head. If she thought about it, she'd go crazy.

"You *have* to think about it, Ellie," Dr. Brenner had told her more than once.

Ellie always had the same response. "When I think about it, I feel as if I'm going to explode or lose my mind. I get so angry."

"It's okay to be angry. It's your *right* to be angry."

"I'm scared I'll lose control. Like before."

"You didn't lose control before, Ellie. He took it from you. He had a knife. Most women—"

"Most women would have fought back."

"You don't know that."

"They wouldn't have begged and pleaded the way I did."

"You were trying to save your life."

"He killed me anyway, Dr. Brenner," she said, tears filling her eyes. "Don't you see? I'm not the person I was. I never will be. I may as well be dead."

Dr. Brenner had taken Ellie's hand that day and held it. "No, Ellie, you won't ever be the same person you were before the attack."

"I feel scared," Ellie had confessed.

"You'll have to take it one day at a time."

Ellie had her doubts. Even now, after months and months of therapy, some of it very painful, she was just as scared and angry and confused as she'd been the day of the attack.

We would be good together, Ellie.

Ellie was still thinking about those words when she climbed into bed a few minutes later and turned out the light. The last thing she saw before she drifted off to sleep was a vision of Cutter Beaumont's handsome face.

• • •

Lord, but she was a pitiful sight, Ellie thought the next morning as she sat on the back steps beside a shrub of golden daisies and drank her first cup of coffee. Mosquito bites covered her arms and legs and made her look as though she were suffering a bad case of the chicken pox. She itched from head to toe, and the red marks running across her limbs were proof that she had scratched herself until her skin was ready to bleed. She had to do something fast.

Ellie dressed quickly in a pair of shorts and a blouse and stuffed her feet into sneakers before locking up the house and heading to the store. She had not noticed the tear in the front porch screen the night before, which was undoubtedly how the mosquitoes had gotten in and all but eaten her alive. Now all she could think of was finding something to stop the itch. She began to walk faster. She was so relieved when she spotted the store, it was all she could do to keep from breaking into a run.

The bell on the door jingled when Ellie shoved it open and made her way inside. She glanced toward the cash register and nodded at the unsmiling woman there. "Hi, what's good for mosquito bites?" she asked, pausing near the front.

Without so much as a nod or a how-do-you-do, the woman made her way around the cash register to the aisle marked TOILETRIES AND MEDICATION. "This lotion should stop the itch," she said, picking up a bottle of pink liquid. She peered over her wire-rimmed glasses at Ellie's arms. "Looks like you got a few chigger bites too. You been in the woods?" She asked the question matter-of-factly but in a judgmental sort of way that suggested if Ellie was stupid enough to be in the woods in the first place she probably *deserved* a few chigger bites.

Ellie remembered cutting through the forest, not only to get to the beach but also Cutter's place. "Yes, I have," she confessed after a moment, half expecting the woman to pull out a ruler and smack her hand with it.

"Well, this is the only thing I have for insect bites. I reckon it's better than nothing."

Ellie didn't think she sounded very optimistic. She wasn't overly friendly either. Probably didn't like outsiders on the island, she thought, then decided she would try and be friendly anyway. It couldn't be easy working next door to Cutter's saloon with all the noise and commotion. That was enough to put anyone in a foul mood. "By the way, I'm Ellie Parks," she said. "I'm staying at the Simmses' house."

"Alma Matthews," the woman replied without a hint of a smile.

"I'm glad to see you're feeling better."

This drew a blank look from the woman. "What do you mean?"

Ellie wished she hadn't said anything. Not only because she didn't want to risk sounding nosy but because she was in such a hurry to get back home and take care of her bites. She had only been trying to exchange a little conversation. "Oh, nothing," she said. "I came by yesterday and someone told me you'd gotten sick and had to go home early."

The woman gave a snort. "Well, whoever told you that was lying," she said. "I ain't never been sick a day in my life. Cutter just told me to take the rest of the day off, so I did."

Ellie forced herself to smile as she picked up her bag. "Oh, well, I must've misunderstood, then. Have a nice day." Without another word, she headed for the front door, pausing to slip her money into her wallet. Someone shoved the door open and, without looking up, she moved aside to finish what she was doing.

"Ellie?"

She would have recognized his voice anywhere. Ellie snatched her head up and found herself looking into Cutter's dark face. It was hard to tell which one of them was more surprised or ill at ease. "Good morning, Sheriff," she said coolly, then moved past him and out the door.

"Ellie, wait—" He followed her.

She could hear his footsteps on the porch behind her. Keeping her eyes straight ahead, Ellie walked as fast as she could.

"Would you wait just a minute, dammit!" Cutter reached for her arm, caught it, and brought her to a skidding halt. "Hey, what's the rush?"

Ellie pulled free, but not before she noted how warm and masculine his hand was. Heat radiated clear up to her arm and shoulder socket. "What do you want? I'm in a bit of a hurry."

"Look, if it's about last night, I'm sorry," he said. "I know I got carried away but—" He frowned. "What the hell happened to your arms and legs? Have you been sitting in red ants?"

"Yes, as a matter of fact, that's *exactly* what I've been doing," she said sarcastically. "Now, if you'll excuse me, I'd like to get home and take care of these bites." She held up her bag. "I have just the thing for them."

"Let me see." He took the bag from her and

looked inside. "This'll help, but I've got something in my first-aid kit that's better."

She grabbed the bag from him. "I think I'll just take my chances with this."

He shrugged as if he didn't care one way or the other. "Go ahead. It can only get worse. Don't come whining to me when they get infected," he added, and started to walk away.

"Is this another one of your lies, Sheriff?" she asked. "Sort of like the lie you told me yesterday about your cashier getting sick?"

Cutter grinned. He'd been caught. "Okay, so I wasn't completely honest. There was no harm done."

"Do you always lie to get what you want?"

"A man has to do what he has to do. Now, you can either hold it against me, or you can take me up on my offer to help you so those bites don't get worse."

"Why'd you do it?"

"Lie about closing the store?" He shrugged. "I wanted you to come to me, and I knew that was the only way. No matter how stubborn and proud, you still had to eat. Maybe you were right about me last night. Maybe I am a bastard. But that's the way I am, and it's not likely I'll change." He paused. "We're a lot alike, you and me."

"How can you possibly say that?"

"We both came to this island seeking refuge from an unpleasant past. It was a long time before these people accepted me. It can get awfully lonely waiting for them to warm up. I could be a good friend to you in the meantime. Now, why don't you come on into the saloon and let me doctor those bites."

She thought about it. Rose had already hinted

that some of the islanders didn't take to new faces. It *would* get lonely if everyone else treated her with the same indifference as the woman in the store. She *did* need a friend. Besides, Cutter had apologized. "Okay," she said at last, then offered him a smile as she followed him into his saloon.

"Have a seat," he told her, motioning toward one of the tables as he went into the back for his first-aid kit. He joined her a moment later. "You've got a few chigger bites as well," he said as he opened the kit. "Let me see your belly button."

"Beg your pardon?"

"Your stomach. Chiggers like to bury themselves beneath your arms, around your navel—" He paused and grinned. "Between your legs. Smart little buggers, if you ask me."

Ellie gave him a withering look. The man never gave up. "Why don't you just give me the medicine, and I'll take it home with me."

"Okay, if you insist." He had hoped she was in enough discomfort to let him apply the ointment personally. "Now, this cream should relieve the itching. Just put it directly on the bites." He reached into the kit and pulled out a bottle of capsules. "This is an antihistamine. It works just as well as anything a doctor can give you."

Ellie took the items and dropped them into her sack. "Thanks," she said. "What do I owe you?"

"It's on the house."

"I insist on paying you."

"Then have me over to dinner tonight."

"No."

"Chicken."

She stood. "I really do have to go."

He followed her to the door and out onto the wooden porch. "I get it. You're playing hard to get, aren't you? I don't mind. I prefer the chase, although I have to confess it's a change from what I'm used to."

Ellie turned and faced him. "You're unbelievable, you know that?"

He grinned. "So I've been told."

If she weren't so frustrated with him she would have laughed out loud. He had to be the most arrogant man she'd ever met. "You don't get it, do you? I don't *want* to spend time with you, Cutter Beaumont. We have nothing in common. When are you going to get that through your thick skull?"

"When you say it like you mean it."

"Oh, for heaven's sake. You really are the most exasperating man I've ever met."

"Should I come around seven o'clock?"

It was that cocky grin that infuriated her so, she decided, and kept her torn between kissing him and slapping it right off his face. That knowledge told her he could be dangerous to her heart. "You are *not* invited, and if you show up, I'm *not* going to let you in. Do you understand?"

He merely stood there, chuckling under his breath as he watched her walk away. What was it going to take to win her over? he wondered. So far, he was getting absolutely nowhere. On a nearby bench two elderly men watched Ellie as well, then glanced at Cutter. He winked. "She's crazy about me."

Five

Two days later, Ellie decided she couldn't put off going to the grocery store any longer, unless she wanted to make a steady diet of boiled eggs and bologna sandwiches.

"You are *not* going to let that big flirt Cutter Beaumont make you a prisoner in this house," she told herself as she brushed her hair and hunted for her old sneakers. Not that she had really minded being holed up in the cozy house for a couple of days. She had spent that time doing things she'd never had time for before, sleeping late and reading. She'd even taken a nap the day before, then gone to bed early with a stack of magazines she'd purchased before coming to the island and a large bag of barbecue-flavor potato chips. For the first time in months she felt totally relaxed. But with it came an ever-increasing sense of restlessness. She had never been one to sit around and do nothing. Except for the brief period she'd been hospitalized after her attack, her life had been full and busy. She had continued to stay busy at work right up to the moment she had taken her leave of absence, but she no longer derived pleasure from it. It had simply become a way to pass the long, lonely hours, hours that needed filling once she began to beg off one date, one social event after another. Until there was almost nobody left in her life. Nobody except her mother. What a grim thought, she told herself.

It was not quite lunchtime when Ellie started down the sandy road toward town. She passed the mail carrier, who stopped his moped and, with a curt nod, handed her a letter. Ellie decided not to be intimidated by his sullen disposition, and the smile she offered in return would have lit up Trump Tower in Manhattan. She glanced at the return address and frowned when she recognized her mother's handwriting. She knew without reading it what it would say. *When are you coming home? Aren't you bored on that island yet? You know you're only making your father's blood pressure go up.* Ellie tucked the letter into her purse and went on her way, waving at those she passed, whether they bothered to return the greeting or not.

Since it was Saturday, several children were out riding bicycles or playing ball in the middle of the road. She noticed Franklin D. standing off to one side all by himself. Pity tugged her heart, and she wondered if the children excluded him from their games because he couldn't talk. When he saw her he broke out in a big grin. She smiled and would have stopped to talk had an older boy not called for him to come home for lunch. Still, Ellie felt better knowing there was at least one person on the island who liked her and was glad she was there. Of course, Cutter seemed content for the moment to have her next door, but she wasn't certain his reasons were entirely honorable.

Once Ellie arrived at the store, she noticed someone had set up a fruit and vegetable stand across the road. She hurried to it, thinking she might purchase some of the fat ripe tomatoes and a cantaloupe.

"Can I help you?" an elderly woman asked.

"Yes, I'd like to buy a carton of these tomatoes." Ellie selected a carton, and the woman transferred them into a paper sack.

"We have fruit and vegetable plants," the woman said, indicating several flats of small plants. "You plan to have a garden this year?"

Ellie glanced in the direction of the plants. She thought about the small plot of rich dirt behind the house. It might be fun to try her hand at planting even if she wouldn't be around to harvest it. "Maybe I will. What do you have?" she asked.

"Oh, we've got tomato plants, cucumber, squash, and zucchini."

"I've never had a garden before," she admitted. "Is it hard?"

"Nothing to it. Just stick the plants in the ground and let Mother Nature do the rest."

Ellie was about to respond when, half turning, something captured her attention. She glanced in the direction of the saloon, where she saw Cutter Beaumont leaning against his Jeep, head cocked to one side, talking to a young woman in a short denim skirt. Although it was impossible to make out what they were saying, the sultry brunette looked at Cutter as if he were something from a dessert cart. Ellie gave a snort of disgust and turned her attention back to the vegetables. Once she had selected a half dozen plants each, the woman running the stand put them in a box for her to carry home. She was in the process of paying for them when someone came up beside her.

"You need help getting those home?" Cutter asked. The look she gave him would have frozen hell over. "Uh-oh," he said. "I knew you'd get mad when you saw me talking to Bitsy Carpenter. Believe me, Ellie, there's nothing between us. She's just a kid."

Ellie could see that he was teasing her, but it just proved what an enormous ego he had. "Don't flatter yourself, Cutter. I don't care if you marry her and spend the rest of your lives on a goat farm. Excuse me." She picked up her box and headed across the street for groceries.

"Here, let me carry that for you," he insisted, grabbing the box before she could object.

"Don't you have more important things to do?" she asked, noting the stares they were drawing. "Surely with all the high school girls home for the day, you can find something to occupy your time." The grin he gave her told her he was getting a huge kick out of her sudden ill manners, and that he was convinced she was jealous. It would never occur to him that she didn't want to be put in the same category as the women who chased after him.

"I'm on my lunch hour," he informed her as he followed her up the steps and through the front door of the grocery. "So we've got plenty of time to chat." Ellie could almost hear the smile in his voice as she grabbed a cart and tried to maneuver it down a narrow aisle, doing her best to ignore him. But it was like trying to ignore a rumbling volcano. She could feel his eyes on her with every move she made, could feel her skin prickling on the back of her neck. She turned and found him staring at her legs. "What are you looking at?"

"Your mosquito bites are better."

She nodded. "Yes, the ointment you gave me worked wonders."

"Is that a thank you?"

She laughed in spite of herself. "Yes, it is."

"Does that mean I'm invited for dinner?"

She dropped the smile and pushed her cart down the aisle. "No. I've already told you—"

"I don't see why we can't be friends, Ellie."

"I think maybe you do."

He put his hand on her arm and stopped her. "Because of an innocent little kiss?"

"Cutter Beaumont, you don't have an innocent bone in your body," she said matter-of-factly. "I know your type, believe me. You're out for one thing."

"At least I'm honest. I don't try to pretend to be something I'm not."

Another laugh. "That's true. You're pretty up-front about being a scalawag."

"See, I make you laugh. I'm good for you, Ellie. You need laughter in your life. You need me."

He really was a handsome devil when he smiled, she decided, and couldn't resist smiling back. "I need you like I need a hole in my head, Cutter Beaumont."

"You need me to give you a ride home," he told her as she continued to fill her cart.

Ellie noted the delight in his voice and gave in. "You're right, I *do* need a ride home. Would you mind?"

"If you'll fix me lunch." When she started to object, he hurried on. "Just a sandwich. A small one."

She sighed, trying to look stern, but it was not an easy task with him standing there grinning from ear to ear, looking every bit like the cat who'd swallowed the canary. Still, it felt good to talk and laugh with someone after two days of solitude. Lord, she must be desperate, she thought, noting his whiskers had grown in those two days. "Okay, I'll make you a sandwich," she said reluctantly. "But only if you'll promise to behave yourself."

Once Ellie paid for her groceries, Cutter carried the sacks to his Jeep and drove her home. "So how do you like the place?" he asked, nodding at the Simmses' house as he pulled into the driveway.

"I love it. All this peace and quiet."

"You don't get bored all alone?"

"No, do you?"

"I don't spend that much time alone."

She blushed as she made her way to the door with a sack. "Stupid question on my part," she said dully.

He threw his head back and laughed. "That's not what I meant. I see people every day in the saloon and at the store."

Ellie paused at her door and unlocked it. "I enjoy being alone." She shoved the door open and walked through, and Cutter followed close behind.

"Yeah, but sooner or later you're going to have to rejoin the human race," he said.

His remark surprised her. "It's not that I'm trying to avoid people, Cutter. But for now, I just want to be alone. To think." She set her bag down and took his.

"I'm not sure that's such a good idea, Ellie. Sometimes, when you dwell on bad times—"

"I'm not trying to *dwell* on anything," she interrupted. "I'm merely trying to work them out in my own mind. Come to terms with what happened so I can go on with my life." She saw the look of skepticism cross his face, as she began to unload the groceries. "Do you have any better suggestions?"

He shrugged. "When something bothers me, I try to keep busy."

"That's just called avoidance behavior. What do you think I've been doing this past year?" She thought of the late nights she'd spent at work. They hadn't helped one iota.

"Well, I don't know the fancy terms for it, but it works for me. Sometimes if I just do something for somebody else, it takes my mind off my problems and makes me feel good."

"I would have never figured you for the Good Samaritan type," she said, and wondered if that was why he'd been so devoted to Mrs. Simms. What was Cutter Beaumont trying to put out of his mind? He'd told her he'd been seeking refuge when he first came to the island. Was he running from something or someone?

He stepped closer and studied her face for a moment. "Yeah, well there's a lot of things you don't know about me."

Ellie felt exposed when he looked at her like that. "I don't want to pry into your business, but you didn't do anything illegal before you came to this island, did you?"

He grinned. "Depends on which side of the law you're standing on, I reckon." He laughed at the shocked look she gave him. "No, I didn't do anything wrong, Miss Priss. I'm not going to let anyone or anything land me in a jail cell, so stop worrying."

Ellie relaxed. For some reason, she believed him. Not because he was above committing a crime but because, even though she hadn't known him long, she did know he would have no qualms about telling her.

Once Ellie had unloaded all the bags and put things away, she prepared several ham-and-cheese sandwiches and opened a bag of chips. Cutter bit into a sandwich and made a production of how good it was. "I just love home cooking," he said, washing it down with a root beer.

"A sandwich is about the closest you're going to come to a home-cooked meal around here," she told him.

"You don't cook?" he asked, looking both shocked and disappointed. "Why didn't you say something before we got involved?"

Ellie was learning she had to overlook a lot of what he said. "I wanted to let you down gently. I couldn't cook an entire meal if my life depended on it."

He looked thoughtful. "I don't know, Ellie. I'm going to have to rethink our relationship. You're not one of those career-minded women who are opposed to anything domestic, are you?" He covered her hand with his own and she raised a quizzical brow. "I know we haven't discussed children, but I want at least three."

Ellie slipped her hand from beneath his, but her hand tingled just from his touch. "Eat your sandwich. I have a lot to do this afternoon."

"Like what?" He looked curious.

"I'm going to plant a garden. Why do you think I bought all those plants?"

"Do you know anything about planting a garden?"

"What's to know? You stick them in the dirt and they grow."

He looked amused. "I'm afraid it's not that simple, Ellie." When she frowned, he went on. "Do you have any cow manure?"

"Not unless I stepped in some."

"See? You have to mix good cow manure in your soil first. But this is your lucky day, because I happen to have several fifty-pound bags in my storeroom."

"Could I buy one from you?"

"I'll do better than that," he told her. "I'll show you how to use it."

"That's really not necessary. If you could just tell me."

He shrugged. "I don't mind. It's the least I can do after this fine lunch you made me."

Ellie was beginning to see a pattern here. Cutter Beaumont was looking for any reason he could find to spend time with her. "Look, all I did was fix you a lousy sandwich for bringing my groceries home. You don't *owe* me anything. Please."

"Then I'll just do it because I'm a nice guy," he said. When she started to object, he silenced her by putting a finger to her lips. "Why don't you stop giving me a hard time and get your tools together, while I go for the manure."

"Tools?"

He reluctantly pulled his finger away and shook his head sadly. "See, you don't even know that you need a rake and a hoe, do you? Oh Ellie, what would you do without me?" He popped the last of his sandwich in his mouth and hurried out the door to his Jeep.

Ellie watched him go, a perplexed frown drawing her brows closely together. She, too, was beginning to worry what she would do without him. And that kind of thinking was dangerous.

Cutter returned a half hour later with a trunk full of tools and the bag of manure and carried them to the backyard. "Here, I bought you a little present," he said, handing her a small sack. She looked inside the bag and found a pair of hot-pink work gloves and several hand tools. "I need all this for a simple vegetable garden?" she asked.

"Nothing is simple when Cutter Beaumont is on the job," he replied. "Where can I change?"

"Change?"

"I had a pair of shorts in my Jeep. You don't expect me to dig a garden in my good clothes, do you?"

Ellie took in his faded jeans and striped pullover. "Oh. You can change in the bathroom." She watched him hurry toward it and close the door. After a moment, she decided she would just go out back and wait for him.

Ellie was not prepared for the likes of Cutter Beaumont in his cutoffs. Bare from the waist up, he strolled out of the house a moment later, adjusting his straw hat to keep the sun out of his eyes. All she could do was stare. The cutoffs were frayed and faded, so ratty looking she was certain they had been wadded up in the back of his Jeep since the previous summer. They were tight and low riding, a good inch below his tan line, below that provocative-looking navel, where the black hair whorled around it and plunged behind a zipper that looked as though he were about to bust right out of it.

"Something wrong?"

Ellie snatched her gaze away from him as

though he'd just tossed hot-pepper sauce in her face. "No. Everything's fine."

"Okay, first we have to get these weeds out. For that we need a rake." Cutter picked up the garden rake, tested the handle between his palms, seemed satisfied, then plunged it into the dirt. "Now, pay close attention," he said.

Ellie stood there with her mouth open as she watched him drag the rake across the rich, black dirt, carrying with it stones and grass and anything else that might be in the way. Standing only a few feet behind him, she watched in awe as the muscles in his arms and back rippled with the effort. She swallowed and found there was not a drop of spit left in her mouth. He turned and smiled, and suddenly there was not even a coherent thought in her head.

"Think you can do it?" he asked.

"Of course I can." Ellie fumbled with her gloves, trying to get them on despite the fact that her hands were trembling. He knows what he's doing, she told herself. He's trying to show off. Strut his stuff. *Well, he can walk around here butt-naked for all I care,* she told herself. *I'm not even tempted.*

Cutter grinned. "Ellie, honey, you've got that glove on the wrong hand."

She glared at him. "I know that. I was just about to pull it off." She finally got them on and reached for her hand tools, then marched down to the other end of the garden and raked for all she was worth.

By the time they had the weeds out, Cutter's back and chest hair glistened with sweat and Ellie's blouse was damp and clinging to her. "Break time," he said, going over to one of the tall oaks and sitting beneath it. He leaned against the trunk and wiped his brow.

"I'll get us something cold to drink," Ellie said, and disappeared inside the house. She came out a moment later carrying two tall glasses of iced tea. She handed him one, and he drank it down without stopping, his Adam's apple bobbing in his throat in a way that held her totally captivated. Ellie took a sip of hers and sat down beside him at a cautious distance. She watched as he reached into the glass for an ice cube and rubbed it across his chest, swirling the thick mass of hair.

"Aw, that feels good," he said, giving her a devilish grin. He met her gaze. "Bet I know what would feel even better."

"What?" It came out sounding like a croak.

"What d'you say we get this garden planted and go swimming?"

"Don't you have to work?"

He shrugged. "Clarence can look after things. Besides, that's the good thing about being in charge. You can do as you please."

She took another sip of her tea, studying him over the rim of her glass. "You like being in charge, don't you?"

"Yes."

"Why?"

"'Cause I don't like taking orders from anybody, that's why. And 'cause I've done enough crummy jobs in my life that I don't intend to do it again."

"What sort of jobs?"

"Everything you can imagine. I've dug ditches and washed cars and mowed grass." He grinned. "And those were the nicer jobs." He sighed and leaned against the tree. "My parents were migrant workers. You ever seen a migrant workers' camp?"

"No."

"Well, you don't want to. I ran away when I was fourteen, because I was afraid I was going to end up just like them. I drifted around a few years, working odd jobs, living from hand to mouth. Finally, I joined the army. Learned to work on helicopters."

"Helicopters?"

He nodded. "See, the only thing I was ever good at was working on cars. I had a choice of working on jeeps or helicopters in the service. There was another guy in there who was real good at it too. We went into business together once Uncle Sam was finished with us." He paused and studied her for a moment. "We sort of invented a part."

"Really? How interesting. Did you make a lot of money?"

All the light went out of his eyes. "Yeah, we made tons of money. That's why I'm here, living a life of luxury." There was a bitter edge to his voice that matched the hard look in his eyes. "But enough about me," he said after a moment. "I want to know more about you."

When Cutter Beaumont didn't want to talk about something he simply changed the subject, and that was that. Ellie tried to think of one thing they might have in common. "Well, I've always enjoyed sports," she began, knowing there wasn't a man alive who didn't enjoy some form of sports.

"Football?"

"Not exactly. I enjoy participating in sports. I used to run a lot. And swim."

"I like to participate too."

"Yeah?"

"Yeah. I like to sit on the sofa and raise a beer to

my mouth every now and then while I watch a good football game."

Ellie laughed. "I like an athletic man."

He adjusted the straw hat on his head so that it was shading his face. "Yeah, well I believe in keeping in shape."

As if to back up that assertion, Ellie took in his broad shoulders, the wide chest. Her gaze drifted downward over his flat stomach and followed his legs. They were lean and brown, feathered with the same black hair that covered the rest of his body.

"Like what you see, Ellie?"

His voice was thick and seductive. Ellie jumped. He was watching her from beneath the brim of his hat. "I was just—"

"Just what? Why don't you admit it, Ellie? You may have been hurt, but I don't think you're ready to live a life of celibacy." She started to get up, but he grabbed her by the wrist, pulling her down. She lost her balance and fell against him. "When are you going to stop running?"

His face was uncomfortably close, so close she could distinguish the brown and black specks in his eyes. Ellie raised her hands automatically to his chest to stop him. Something in her stomach fluttered when her palm came into contact with the hard muscle beneath his still sweaty skin. He was solid as concrete. "Look, I've already told you—"

"I know what you told me, Ellie, but I don't believe a word of it. You're a beautiful young woman with your whole life ahead of you. You can't just curl up and die because of what one man did to you."

Ellie stared back, speechless as Cutter spoke,

his voice soft as a summer breeze. The teasing smile he usually had for her had been replaced with a look of pure tenderness. She was vaguely aware that he still held her fast. As he talked, he drew invisible circles on her inner wrist, his touch mesmerizing her as much as his deep voice. "You don't understand—" she began.

"I understand more than you know. You don't hold the patent on pain, Ellie. Everybody gets knocked around in this life. But I'm here now. Let me kiss away that pain." Without another word, he ducked his head and touched her lips lightly with his own, so lightly, Ellie imagined she had been brushed by a butterfly's wing. Her eyes fluttered closed. She held her breath as he kissed her again, this time lingeringly, as he pulled her onto his lap.

All at once Ellie was half lying in his lap, staring at him with her heart in her eyes. She trembled in his arms. She was standing at the crossroads of passion and fear. She wanted to trust him so badly and put an end to the loneliness that she had created with her own self-imposed isolation. She longed to share with him the intimacies that other couples shared and fill up those hollow places inside that had been with her so long. "Cutter?" Her voice quavered.

She sounded small and vulnerable, almost childlike. Cutter gazed down at Ellie, thinking she had never looked more desirable, with her blouse clinging to her, her shorts riding high on her thighs. He wanted her so badly, he hurt. And he knew, with just a little prodding, he could have her. He could see it in her face. She was *almost* willing. A few kisses would send her over the edge. He was ready and able and hard. "Ellie?" He touched her face, stroked her cheek, and followed the outline of her mouth with trembling fingers. Once more he met her gaze. The trust he saw there almost choked him. He wasn't sure how it had happened, and he knew damn good and well he didn't deserve it. The only thing he knew for certain was that he couldn't bear to hurt her, not after what she had already been through.

Cutter raised his eyes to the heavens and sighed. Later he would kick his butt all the way to town and back, but he would rather put a gun to his head than cause more emotional damage to the woman in his arms. "We'd best get back to that garden," he said, raising her up and setting her away from him. Her dazed look turned to utter confusion, and Cutter forced himself to glance away. It was one thing to go after a woman just for the fun of it, but it was another thing altogether to take advantage of someone who was, at the moment, so utterly defenseless. Springing to his feet, he stalked toward the garden with a vengeance, determined to work until he dropped. Or at least until he stopped thinking about what he wanted to do to Ellie Parks.

Six

It took almost two hours to prepare the garden and set out the plants, during which time Ellie and Cutter exchanged very few words. She had never been so uncomfortable in her life, not to mention downright embarrassed. Finally, Cutter raised up, dusted his hands off on the back of his shorts, and pronounced them finished.

"It's the nicest garden I've ever seen," Ellie said, still unable to make eye contact with the man now that she'd literally thrown herself at him. She couldn't imagine what he thought of her. The first time he'd kissed her, she had chewed him out and ordered him to stay away from her. This time she'd been all over him. "Would you like another glass of iced tea?" she asked as she gathered up the tools.

Cutter didn't miss the anxiety in her voice. If things had been tense before, they were worse now that he'd kissed her a second time. Why couldn't he keep his blasted hands to himself? he wondered. After knowing all she'd been through,

81

he had no business trying to romance her. Even if she *had* seemed half willing to kiss him back, he wasn't at all qualified to deal with her emotional struggles. And he knew Ellie Parks well enough to know that when a man took her to bed, he was going to have a whole slew of emotions on his hands. That was the last thing he needed in his life.

"I can't stay," he said after a moment. "I need to clean up and get back to the saloon."

Ellie fidgeted with one of her soiled work gloves. She didn't know whether to hate him or feel grateful toward him for calling things to a halt. The only thing she did know for certain was that she was more confused than she had been in a long time. What business did she have throwing herself at a man like Cutter Beaumont, anyway? Unless she was just looking to get hurt again. It was one thing to want to rejoin the human race and start dating once more, but she needed to cut her teeth on a nice, respectable sort of man and stay as far away as possible from the likes of Cutter.

"Well, thanks for all you've done," she said, intent on dismissing him now that she was thinking rationally. "I know it's silly for me to plant a garden when I won't even be here to watch it come in. Perhaps you'll look after it when I'm gone. I expect you to help yourself to the vegetables when they're ready."

"That's very neighborly of you," he told her.

"Don't be silly. It's the least I can do after all you've done for me."

She didn't want to be indebted to him. He didn't blame her. "Thanks, I'll remember that. See you around, Ellie." Then, with a quick nod, he made his way to the front of the house and climbed into his Jeep.

Ellie was still thinking about Cutter and the kiss when someone knocked on her door that evening. She froze at the kitchen sink where she had been washing her dinner dishes. Finally, she dried her hands on a kitchen towel and made her way to the front of the house. She smiled when she found Rose and Franklin D. at her front door.

"Evenin'," Rose said. "You like blackberry cobbler? Me and Franklin D. picked a mess of berries behind our house, and I been bakin' all day."

"I love cobbler," Ellie told her as she let them in. "And I have just the thing to go on it. But you and Franklin D. have to join me."

Rose grinned down at her son. "That's what we were hoping she'd say, right, boy?" Franklin D. nodded at his mother and grinned.

Ellie led the two visitors to the kitchen, where she served them each a bowl of the still-warm cobbler, topped with a generous scoop of the vanilla ice cream she'd bought at the store that day. She tasted a spoonful and closed her eyes in obvious pleasure. "It's heavenly, Rose," she said. "And very thoughtful of you to bring it."

"Oh, it's nothing. We got enough blackberries out back to feed everybody on the island. The weather's been so nice they came out early this year."

"Which reminds me, I have something to show you." Ellie waited until they had finished eating before she led her guests out to her garden. "What do you think?" she said, pointing to the neat rows of vegetable plants.

Rose looked impressed. "I thought you said you didn't know nothing about gardening."

Ellie blushed. "I had a little help."

"Oh, yeah? Let me guess. Cutter Beaumont?"

Ellie looked surprised. "How'd you know?"

Rose chuckled. "Cutter would cut trees down with his teeth if it meant spending time with a pretty woman."

Ellie smiled shyly. "Yes, well, I pretty much had him pegged for a big flirt from the beginning."

"You just watch yourself around that man," Rose said teasingly. "He's broken more hearts than I can shake a stick at." A breeze whispered through the trees. "Looks like it might rain," she said. "The weather gets crazy this time of year, we never know what to expect. C'mon, Franklin D., we'd best get home, just in case. Be dark soon anyway." She took her son's hand, then paused. "By the way, I was thinking you might like to go to church with me and my boys tomorrow. My husband works Sundays, so he can't go. Anyway, there'll be a picnic out back of the church afterward. Folks usually bring something."

"I'm not much of a cook," Ellie said.

"Don't matter. I fried two chickens today. That's plenty."

"I'd love to go with you."

"Good. We'll come by for you 'round ten-thirty."

Ellie thanked her again for the cobbler, then watched the two take the road toward home as the first droplets of rain began to fall.

Ellie was ready and waiting when Rose and her boys knocked on the front door the following morning. Dressed in a neat cotton shift with her hair tied back in a scarf, Ellie joined them, a plate of chocolate covered donuts in her hands. "I didn't want to come empty-handed," she told Rose.

"This here's my oldest boy, Booker T.," Rose said, motioning to the boy standing beside Franklin D. Both boys were dressed in neat slacks and crisp white dress shirts with bow ties. "Booker T., show some manners and carry that plate for Miss Parks. And don't you dare drop it in the sand." The boy hurried forward and took the plate of donuts from Ellie, smiling shyly at her as he did so.

"Nice to meet you, Booker T.," Ellie said.

"Same here, ma'am," he mumbled.

"We ain't got time for pleasantries this morning," Rose said matter-of-factly as she adjusted the mauve scarf she'd tied around her hair. "We were late leaving the house this morning."

"I'm ready," Ellie said, noting how attractive Rose looked in her print dress. Her coffee-color skin was smooth and unblemished, her figure tall and slender.

They started down the road. "You'll like Reverend Newman," Rose said as they neared the small white church flanked by tall red-tipped hedges. "He's not one of those fire-and-brimstone preachers who holler and carry on and scare the young'uns."

"Is this the only church on the island?" Ellie asked, noting the large crowd gathered out front.

Rose nodded and waved at several people as they passed. "Yes. But if you're lookin' to run into Cutter Beaumont, don't count on it."

Ellie's face flamed. "I never—"

"Don't tell me you weren't thinkin' it," Rose said with a knowing look. "I can see those pretty green eyes of yours flittin' around in your head. Not that

I blame you, of course. A man with his looks." She grinned at the shocked look on Ellie's face. "But don't worry. He'll be here for the picnic later. Funny how he and Clarence are too busy for church services, but they always find time to eat afterward."

Reverend James Newman was a small-framed man with tortoiseshell-rimmed glasses and a balding head who smiled brightly at Ellie when Rose introduced her at the door. "We're so glad to have you in our little church, Miss Parks," he said. "I hope you'll join us each Sunday while you're on the island."

Ellie assured him she would, then followed Rose into the narthex, where they set their plates on a large table holding other dishes. Finally, they stepped inside the chapel and found seats. Rose waved to various people, introduced Ellie to those closest to them, then sat back and waited for the reverend to take his place at the altar.

After the service the women claimed their dishes from the front room, and the congregation moved to the picnic area out back. While they got things ready, the men stood off to one side talking and smoking. The children chased one another on the wide lawn.

Ellie had never seen so much food in one place. There were casseroles and vegetable dishes and desserts galore, not to mention a veritable mountain of fried chicken, biscuits, and corn muffins. She was almost embarrassed to uncover the plate of donuts she'd brought.

"Why Miz Parks, I'll bet you made those donuts from scratch, didn't you?"

Ellie would have recognized that voice any-where. She snapped her head up and found herself looking into Cutter Beaumount's laughing black eyes. She offered him a saccharine smile. "Yes, Sheriff, as a matter of fact, I did."

He plucked a donut from the plate and studied it. "They look as nice as anything you can buy in a store," he said.

"Rose was right," Ellie mumbled. "She said you'd be here for the picnic, even if you didn't make it to church."

"Smart woman, that Rose," he said with a wink. Then, as Reverend Newman stepped closer, Cutter cleared his voice and tried to look serious. "Actually, Clarence and I had to tend to some important business before we could come. I hate that we missed the service."

"Cutter Beaumont, you're a lyin' dog," Rose said once the minister shook hands with Cutter and made his way toward a group of elderly women. "You and my brother are just a couple of heathens, that's what you are."

Clarence Davis ambled toward them. "Rose, are you talking 'bout me behind my back again?" he asked, pausing to grab a chicken leg from her plate.

She gave a snort. "I didn't say anything I wouldn't say to your face, little brother."

"Where's that ugly husband of yours?" he asked.

"On his shrimp boat, where else?"

"You know what they say about all work and no play, big sister?"

Rose patted him on the cheek. "Who says we don't do our share of playing, honey bunches?"

Ellie laughed at the teasing display between brother and sister, then turned her gaze to Cutter who was laughing as well. Their gazes locked for one breathless moment, and she knew he was thinking about that kiss the day before. Ellie was thankful when Rose asked her to prepare a plate for Franklin D. and she was forced to concentrate on the boy. The less she thought about Cutter Beaumont and his kisses, the better.

The afternoon turned out to be one of the happiest Ellie had spent in a long time. She held babies, talked with the older islanders who'd been on Erskine all their lives, and visited with other young mothers whom Rose introduced her to.

Alma Matthews, the clerk from Cutter's store, inquired about Ellie's chigger bites in her matter-of-fact way. But all the while, Ellie was aware of every move Cutter made. She watched him toss a football to the boys, saw him push the little girls on the old rusted swings, and noticed every time one of the women talked to him.

"Oh, would you just look at that Bitsy Carpenter making eyes at the sheriff?" a woman at the next table said loud enough for Ellie to hear. "I wish Cutter wouldn't encourage her. She's just a child."

Rose pursed her lips. "Cutter doesn't have to encourage her, Margaret. Bitsy's always been a wild hare, chasin' everything in britches. If she was *my* daughter . . ."

Ellie didn't want to hear any more. She didn't want to know the names of all the women who'd thrown themselves at Cutter, and be reminded that she had done the same thing the day before. She took Franklin D. by the hand and led him to the edge of the woods where they picked wildflowers. Afterward, he fell asleep in her lap at the picnic table.

Finally, it was time to go. Rose tried to wake her

son, but he merely snuggled closer to Ellie. "I'll carry him," Ellie said, even as Rose protested that he was too heavy.

"He's fine," Ellie assured her as they started down the dirt road toward home.

Rose nudged her. "Aren't you going to say good-bye to Cutter?" she whispered.

Ellie blushed. "No."

The other woman laughed softly. "I don't blame you. I wouldn't want to have to stand in line for a man's attention, either."

Ellie carried Franklin D. all the way home, although Rose claimed she was spoiling him rotten by doing so. But the boy was sleeping so soundly, Ellie didn't have the heart to wake him. They finally arrived at a neat frame house, and Rose led Ellie inside and to a bedroom decorated with play army men. Very gently, Ellie laid the boy down on his bed and covered him.

"Stay and have a cup of coffee with me," Rose said, once she'd closed the door to the boy's room. "My husband won't be home for several more hours. I'll be glad when he can stop working seven days a week."

Ellie was only too glad to stay for a while. She liked Rose's house, with its ruffled curtains and gingham tablecloth. "Thanks for inviting me to go with you today," she said once the woman had poured their coffee and joined her at the table. "I had a wonderful time." She also suspected it was because of Rose that the other islanders had been so friendly.

"Oh, you're welcome to go with us anytime."

"Yes, but you're going to have to teach me how to fry chicken."

"Ain't nothin' to it, honey. By the time your vacation is over, you'll be a whiz in the kitchen."

"I'll miss this place when I have to go back," Ellie told her, wondering how she could have gotten so attached to the island in just a few short days. "I'll miss the peace and quiet."

"You mean you'll miss Cutter," Rose said.

Ellie shifted in her chair. "There's nothing between us."

"Uh-huh." The woman didn't look at all convinced.

For some reason it was important to Ellie to make Rose believe her. "Look, I'll be the first to admit he's a handsome devil, but I'd be a fool to get involved with a man like him. You yourself said he's broken a lot of hearts."

"Yes, but I have a feelin' he's met his match with you, Ellie Parks."

Ellie gazed at the woman. "You don't understand. I don't want to . . ." She paused. She wasn't ready to talk about her attack.

"You don't want to get hurt," Rose said. "Isn't that what you were about to say?" When Ellie nodded, she went on. "Well, I can tell you this, neither does Cutter."

"Which explains why he chases everything in skirts," Ellie said, sarcasm slipping into her voice.

Rose took her hand. "He might chase them, honey, but he makes sure nobody gets caught. Yet. But if you want my opinion, I think all that's about to change."

"I'm only here for a short period of time, Rose. I've got a life waiting for me back in Savannah. I've got family and friends and a career." She tried to imagine what her cultured friends would make of a man like Cutter Beaumont. Her mother would have a fit.

"Shoot," Rose said, waving off the remark. "That don't mean nothing. You find the right man, and you won't care about none of that."

Ellie leaned close. "I can assure you. Cutter Beaumont with his unshaved face and coon dogs is not that man for me."

"We'll see about that."

Seven

For the next few days Ellie concentrated on getting Mrs. Simms's yard in shape. She found an old lawn mower in the back shed that actually worked, then spent the entire day cutting and raking the tall grass. Afterward she sipped iced tea on the front steps and listened to the crickets, delighting in the cool breeze and the sweet smell of freshly cut grass. She had never known such peace.

The next day she pulled weeds and clipped hedges, then in the late afternoon walked to the store and bought several packets of seeds—daisies, morning glory, and pansies. She saw Cutter's Jeep parked beside the saloon, but the man himself was nowhere in sight.

"Nose is gettin' blistered," Alma Matthews said as she rang up Ellie's sale.

"I beg your pardon?"

"I said your nose is gettin' blistered from too much sun," the woman repeated, peering over the rim of her glasses at Ellie. "Better put somethin' on it." It came out sounding more like an order than a concerned request.

"Thanks, Mrs. Matthews, I will." Ellie made her way out of the store, telling herself she was not disappointed she hadn't run into Cutter.

The next day she was up early planting seeds and attending the plants in her garden. When she wasn't performing chores, she took long walks on the beach and explored the island. Still, she never once caught sight of Cutter. She began to suspect he was avoiding her, then decided it had something to do with that kiss, the same kiss that had started her thinking of him in a romantic way.

Of course, it was totally and completely insane to think of him in that way. It wasn't as if they had a whole lot in common.

So why had he backed off when it had become obvious she might enjoy his kisses, after all? Hadn't he been waiting for just such an opportunity? She couldn't figure it. And then, just as she was about to give up on his reasons, it hit her. It obviously had to do with her rape. Ellie stood there, immobilized as she considered it. Perhaps, as he'd been holding her in his arms, Cutter had thought about the man who'd attacked her only a year before. Some men simply couldn't deal with rape. Hadn't she learned that from the support group she had attended? Was Cutter one of those men who would see her as defiled or sullied material? Ellie was suddenly reminded of the middle-aged woman in her support group who'd cried when she had told the others how her husband had been unable to make love to her after the rape. Everyone in the group had cried along with her.

It hurt to think that Cutter might indeed find her repulsive now that he knew the truth. It also made her angry as hell. Just who did he think he was, to pass judgment on her for something that she hadn't been able to control? And if that wasn't the reason he was avoiding her, then what was?

One afternoon, when she'd been on the island a little more than a week, Ellie was in the process of checking her mail when she spied Franklin D. and Booker T. walking toward her house with what looked to be the ugliest dog she'd ever laid eyes on. Ellie smiled and waved as she pulled out the lone envelope bearing her mother's handwriting. She winced as she thought of the last letter sitting on her night table, still unanswered. "Hello boys," she said. "Where'd you get that handsome animal?"

"You want this dog, Miss Parks?" Booker T. asked without preamble. "I know he ain't much to look at, but our daddy says he's goin' to shoot him if he catches him at the house one more time."

Ellie gazed at the mangy-looking mutt, who looked and smelled as though he hadn't been bathed in months. She'd thought Cutter's dogs were ugly, but they'd win beauty contests next to this one. "I'm sorry," she said, "but I'm only going to be on the island for a few weeks. I'm sure you can find someone to take him, though."

Booker T. shook his head. "I done asked everyone. Nobody wants a dog that looks like this."

Ellie noted sadly that the animal's ribs were poking through his flesh. "Has he eaten anything?"

"Oh yeah, I've been feeding him twice a day. He's just skinny. Skinny and ugly. That's what we been calling him. Ugly."

Ellie laughed softly. "Did you check to see if Mr. Beaumont wanted him? I understand he's an animal lover."

"Cutter says he already has too many dogs."

"Well, that's true," she mumbled, remembering the nights she'd lain awake once Cutter's dogs started barking and woke her. "Your father won't really shoot him, though," she said doubtfully. "Maybe if you explain—"

"You don't know our daddy," Booker T. told her. Beside him, Franklin D. nodded soberly.

Ellie was torn as to what to do. The last thing she needed at the moment was a dog on her hands. But the thought of someone harming the animal was more than she could stand. "Why don't you leave him with me," she suggested, "and I'll ask Mr. Beaumont to reconsider once he gets home from work. If he doesn't want the dog, I'll try to find someone else to take him." She remembered the bulletin board at the store where people listed items they had for sale. Maybe she would run a notice. Of course, she'd have to bathe the animal first. Nobody was going to take him in his present state.

Booker T. looked relieved as he handed her the rope tied to the dog's skinny neck. "I know he don't smell too good, but Mama won't let us bring him in the house for a bath."

Ellie gazed into the dog's soulful brown eyes and felt her sympathy stirred. Cutter would take him, she was certain. Nobody with half a heart could turn his back on an animal like that. "What have you been feeding him?"

"Just table scraps. I may as well warn you he eats a lot."

"It must go straight through him," she said, noting the swaybacked spine that gave him the appearance of an old workhorse.

"Well, we'd best get back to the house," Booker

T. said. "Thanks for takin' the dog, ma'am." The boys turned to go. Suddenly, Franklin D. hurled himself at the pitiful animal and hugged him tightly.

"Franklin D. was attached to that ol' mutt," Booker T. said, clucking his teeth sadly.

Ellie knelt beside the younger boy and slipped her arms around his narrow waist. He was as skinny as the dog. "It's okay, Franklin D.," she said softly. "I'll find him a good home. Maybe the new owners will let you visit."

Booker T. had to literally drag his tearful brother away. Ellie watched them go, feeling sorry for the little boy. Once the two brothers disappeared around a bend of trees, she looked down at the dog. "You know I'm going to have to give you a bath," she said. "I can't possibly find you a home when you smell like you've been sleeping in cow manure." The dog stared back at her dumbly.

Ellie led the animal across the yard and onto the porch. "Now, mind your manners," she said, "and don't you dare mess on Mrs. Simms's rug." Ellie chuckled at the one-sided conversation she was having with the sad-eyed beast. "Lord, it's pitiful to be this desperate for someone to talk to. Come on, straight to the bathroom with you."

It was no easy job bathing the dog, Ellie discovered. Just getting the scrawny animal into the old-fashioned bathtub was a feat in itself. He suddenly turned scared on her and did his level best to get back out, clawing the sides of the porcelain tub as though afraid she were going to drown him.

"Sit!" Ellie told him in an authoritative tone.

Finally the dog settled down. It took more than an hour to bathe him, considering the fact that

Ellie had to scrub him three times, using an entire bottle of her best shampoo. Each time she let the water out, it just seemed to get blacker. At last, she dried him off and studied him. His brown color had lightened considerably, but he was still a drab, dull shade.

"Well, you don't look much better, but you definitely smell better. Now all we've got to do is think of a name for you. Something noble," she added, wishing he would hold his head up. He was without a doubt the most pathetic creature she'd ever laid eyes on.

"I'll call you Duke," she decided after a moment. "That's a grand name if ever there was one."

The dog yawned and hunkered down on the floor.

The sun was beginning to set as Ellie led Duke toward Cutter's place, taking the long way down the dirt road instead of cutting through the woods and risking more chigger bites. She had to admit she was a little nervous at the thought of seeing him again, but she had to find the dog a home. Besides, she wanted to know where they stood as friends. If Cutter Beaumont was going to reject her over something that had happened in her past, then he was no friend to begin with. A cool breeze rustled the trees, and she glanced up at the sky where one section had grown dark. It looked as though it might rain. Rose had told her the weather was unpredictable this time of year. She quickened her steps. When she arrived at Cutter's double-wide she saw his Jeep sitting out front and could hear "Here's a Quarter (Call Someone Who Cares)" by Travis Tritt blaring from his open windows. She had to knock twice before he answered.

"Ellie." He looked surprised to see her when he opened the door.

He was wearing the floral shirt he'd worn the day she'd met him in the saloon trying to ward off Clovis Henry's blows. "I hope I didn't come at a bad time," she said.

He shook his head. "I just got in." His gaze drifted to the dog. "Don't tell me Booker T. convinced you to take that ugly mutt off his hands." He chuckled.

"What's wrong with him?" Ellie said. "I think Duke is a fine animal."

"Duke?" He burst into laughter. After seeing the expression on her face, he tried to look serious. "Is that why you cleaned him up and brought him over here?" he asked. "So I'd take him off your hands?"

Ellie pretended to look shocked, although she knew better than to attempt to pull the wool over Cutter Beaumont's eyes. But that didn't stop her from trying. "Okay, I might as well level with you," she said. "I was thinking about keeping him myself, seeing what a great pet he'd make, but when I heard what an excellent coon dog he was, I thought maybe you'd—"

Once again he laughed. "Coon dog? That dog wouldn't know the difference between a coon and a two-headed mule."

"That's not true," Ellie said. "I understand he's a wonderful hunter."

"Great, why don't we try him out?"

"I beg your pardon?"

"I'm going coon hunting tonight. You can bring your dog and go with me."

At first she thought he was kidding, but the look on his face told her he was dead serious. "Me go coon hunting?" she said in disbelief. "You must be out of your mind. I don't get a major thrill out of watching some poor animal torn to bits by a bunch of dogs."

"I don't let the dogs kill the coon," Cutter told her. "We just do it for the chase. Once we get a coon treed I back them off and start on a new trail."

It sounded about as exciting as having her head shaved, but if it meant she might convince him to take the dog, it was worth it. Otherwise, she was going to spend the next couple of days going door-to-door to find the dog a home. She was already beginning to regret her decision to take him in the first place. "Okay, I'll go," she said a bit reluctantly. "Unless it rains. I noticed clouds—"

"They'll blow over by the time we go. You want a cold beer?"

He was inviting her in. He hadn't even bothered to see if she was alive the past few days, and now he was asking her in for a cold beer. She didn't get it. "No thanks," she told him. "What time should I plan to meet you?"

"I'll pick you up around ten. Be sure to wear long pants to keep the chiggers away. You might want to spray yourself with repellent while you're at it."

"Believe me, I will. Is there anything else I need to bring?"

"No, I've got plenty of supplies." Cutter glanced from her to the dog. "By the way, what are you feeding him?"

"I gave him half a package of hot dogs before I came over."

"That could get expensive. I'll bring a bag of dry dog food when I come."

Ellie thanked him and made the walk back to her house, leading Duke with the rope. Although she thought Cutter had looked pleased to see her, he hadn't flirted like before. If anything, he seemed restrained. Ellie pondered it. She didn't want this tension between them. She realized that she had enjoyed Cutter's teasing, and now she missed it.

Ellie felt a few droplets of rain on her arms, but when they stopped she decided Cutter knew what he was talking about when he said it would all blow over. At the house she made herself a light meal and dressed in her oldest jeans, then spent the remainder of the time reading one of the books she'd brought.

Cutter arrived precisely at ten, dressed in jeans and a long-sleeve cotton shirt. "You ready?" he said. "My dogs are having a fit to get started."

"Just give me a second." Ellie grabbed her keys while Cutter slipped a collar and leash around Duke's neck, looking amused as he did so. "Yes, Ellie, this looks like a real good hunting dog." Duke yawned and scratched his ear as though wishing he could just stay behind and go back to his nap.

"Remember what they say about not being able to judge a book by its cover," she told him, slipping a cotton sweater over her T-shirt. "Okay, I'm ready."

Cutter led her dog out to the Jeep and put him in the back with two large blueticks, who were pacing the small area like restless zoo animals. "Settle down, boys, and don't hurt this old fellow," he said. "He can't help it if he's ugly."

"You're going to give that poor animal an inferiority complex," Ellie called back from her seat.

Cutter climbed into the Jeep a moment later and started the engine. He drove to the other side of the island, where he claimed the woods were thickest. Once he parked, he strapped a light around Ellie's head and handed her a canteen. "Just in case you get thirsty," he told her as he strapped a light to his own forehead. "Here, spray yourself with this. It'll keep the bugs off."

Ellie sprayed her clothes while Cutter pulled the dogs out of the back of the Jeep. The two blueticks strained against their leashes, while her dog just sat there and looked bored. Cutter shook his head sadly. "Here, you take him," he said, handing her the leash. "I don't want to be seen with him." He ignored the dark look she shot him as they started for the woods.

"Now, you promise the dogs won't hurt the coon, right?" Ellie said, keeping close to Cutter. She had never seen such darkness. It looked as if everything was wrapped in black velvet.

"Nobody's going to get hurt, Ellie." He paused. "Okay, let's let 'em go." He freed his dogs and they raced off and disappeared through the brush.

Ellie unleashed Duke. "Go boy!" she said. "Go find that coon." The dog simply sat there with a dumb look on his face. "Go on, boy!" she repeated more firmly.

"I don't think he's interested in finding a coon tonight," Cutter said dryly.

"Give him a chance," she said. "It's his first time."

Cutter arched both brows. "I thought you said he was a good hunter."

Ellie realized she'd been caught in a bold-faced

lie. "He *is* a good hunter, but he's used to tracking bears."

Cutter let out a whoop of laughter. "You're trying to tell me this is a bear-hunting dog?"

Ellie tried to keep a straight face. "You don't see any bears hanging around, do you?"

Grinning from ear to ear, Cutter slung one arm over her shoulder. "I would like to compliment you, Ellie."

"Oh?"

"Yes. I consider myself somewhat of an expert at bending the truth, and I can tell you have great potential."

Ellie gazed at him for a moment, thinking he had never looked more handsome and rugged. The checkered cotton shirt he wore was a change from the floral-print shirts she was used to seeing him in, but she decided he would look sexy wearing burlap. He shifted slightly, and Ellie saw him lower his head. The smile disappeared, and his look softened. He was going to kiss her, and she was going to let him. She raised her head as his mouth covered hers. Something fluttered deep in her stomach as their lips made contact, warm in the night air, his coaxing a response from her. Her lips parted and he was inside, exploring the recesses of her mouth, branding her with the fiery touch of his tongue. Ellie kissed him back, giving herself freely to the magic of his slow, drugging kiss. And then, all at once, she was in his arms, pressed tightly against his solid chest. The kiss deepened, and she was filled with a strange new excitement. Her pulse raced as his musky scent enveloped her. It was as intoxicating as the taste of his tongue. He was so stunningly virile and sexy that her head spun. Ellie grasped the front of his shirt and held on tight.

Finally, he raised his head and gazed at her for a long silent moment. He raised his thumb to her lips and traced the bow shape. "You kissed me back this time, Ellie," he said softly.

"Yes, I did, didn't I?" She smiled and he returned it, and for a moment all the tension was gone between them, replaced with a strong sense of camaraderie and deep caring. Ellie could see it in his eyes, feel it emanating from his big body.

Then, suddenly and without warning, the dogs let out loud, high-pitched barks, one right after the other. Ellie jumped.

"Strike!" Cutter said, breaking out into a smile.

Ellie blinked. "Huh?"

"They found themselves a coon. Let's go." He grabbed her hand and headed in the direction of the noise.

It was all she could do to keep up with Cutter's long-legged gait as they hurried through the woods. There was a loud screeching sound that made the hairs stand up on the back of Ellie's neck. She came to an abrupt halt. "What was that?"

"The coon," Cutter said, tugging her once more. "It's okay. He's just having a little conversation with my dogs."

Ellie shuddered when she heard the sound again, echoing through the trees. "I don't like it, Cutter."

He didn't slow his pace. "It's okay, honey. They can't get to the coon." Cutter reached for the extra flashlight strapped to his belt and shined it through the brush so they could get a better look. Finally they spotted the dogs, yapping and hollering and doing their level best to climb the tall tree. "Look up there," he said, shining his light. "You can see the coon's eyes."

Ellie fixed her gaze on the upper branches of the tree where she could barely make out the animal. When Cutter moved the light away, the coon's eyes glittered in the darkness. The animal let out another shuddering screech. "The dogs are scaring him, Cutter," she said. "Call them off."

"Aw, that coon ain't scared, honey. He's mad. He'd sooner tear off a hound's face than look at him." Cutter shone his light back on the tree, and the animal tried to duck from it. "He's a big one."

Ellie watched the black-and-gray animal scurry across a branch as though looking for a place to hide. She didn't like it. Not because she felt the coon was in any physical danger, but because she didn't like to think of an animal being scared. She sensed the fear in the coon and knew its heart was probably pounding right out of his chest. She knew firsthand what it was like to feel trapped, as though there was no way out. And then she watched in dread as the coon climbed to a higher limb and teetered there for several long, agonizing seconds. She saw the limb bend, heard it crack. The coon lost its balance and fell, hitting the ground with a dull, sickening thud. Ellie heard a scream, then realized it was her own as the hounds pounced on the animal.

Cutter muttered a string of curses and ran to his dogs, trying to pull them off. Ellie was right behind him, screaming and pleading for him to hurry. But it was too late.

"Oh, God!" Ellie's hands flew to her face.

Cutter reached for her. "Ellie, listen. That coon was dead when he hit the ground."

She shook him off. "You don't know that!"

"If he wasn't dead, he was at least unconscious. He never knew what hit him."

"You have absolutely no way of knowing that," she said, then realized she was yelling. "You lied to me. You told me the dogs wouldn't kill anything."

"Well, how in the hell was I supposed to know the damn stupid coon was going to fall out of the tree? I've never—"

"You're a liar and a murderer!"

"Ellie, get a grip on yourself!" He grabbed her once more and shook her slightly.

Her mind was spinning. Ellie shoved Cutter away and turned in the direction from where they'd come. All she could think of was that poor coon. She started to run. She was crying, sobbing actually. Behind her, Cutter yelled for her to stop but she didn't even slow down. A low-hanging limb hit her in the head and knocked the light off, but she kept moving nevertheless. She heard Duke right behind her. Somehow, miraculously, she found the road and followed it, letting the moon guide her with its dim light. In the distance she heard Cutter calling for her, heard his Jeep, saw his headlights on the road. She ducked behind a tree and waited for him to pass before taking to the road again.

At some point it began to drizzle. The air was heavy with moisture. Ellie touched her face and found it wet, but she didn't know if it was from the rain or her tears. She didn't care. All she cared about was finding her way back, out of the dark and the looming shadows.

Cutter searched for Ellie for twenty minutes before the heavens opened up and it began to rain in earnest. He circled back, wondering if he had somehow missed her, but there was no sight of her anywhere. He cursed again. With her luck, she'd get lost and never find her way out of that thicket. A flash of lightning lit up the sky.

Back at his place, Cutter got the dogs out of the truck and to their pens where they ran for shelter. He slammed the gate and raced back to the Jeep for all he was worth, knowing he had to find Ellie, no matter what. Where could she be? he wondered, as he took to the road again, shining his flashlight in the trees. He parked, climbed out of the Jeep and called her name at the top of his lungs while the cold rain stung his face and eyes and soaked his clothes. He should have his head examined for taking her with him, he told himself as he remembered the horror on her face when his dogs attacked the coon. He closed his eyes because he couldn't stand thinking about how she'd looked at him, as though he were the lowest thing on earth.

It was the first time he could remember caring what anybody, especially a woman, thought of him.

Cutter climbed back into his Jeep and drove on as the rain pounded his windshield and all but obscured the road from view. Another bolt of lightning lit up the sky, followed by a crack of thunder so loud, it seemed as if the ground would split open from the force. He sped toward the Simmses' house, not knowing where else to look. If Ellie wasn't there, he would go to the saloon and arrange a search party.

Cutter tried not to think of all the things that could happen to her in the woods in the middle of what looked like was going to be a downright nasty thunderstorm. He sighed and wiped his wet face with the back of his hand.

He had the antidote for snake bites in his first-aid kit, but it wouldn't do Ellie a bit of good out there. Fear gnawed at his gut as he thought of the poisonous snakes he'd seen on the island over the years. And then, with another flash of lightning, he saw her: walking down the edge of the road in the rain, still clutching the leash that held that pitiful looking mongrel of hers. Cutter was dizzy with relief as he gunned the engine and headed toward her.

"Ellie!" He slowed the Jeep beside her. "Ellie, get in," he ordered. "You're wetter than a drowned monkey. Come on, honey. I'll take you home." She ignored him and continued on her way. In a fit of frustration, Cutter slammed the gears into park and jumped out of the idling Jeep. Ellie bolted forward, but he was faster. He grabbed her and hauled her kicking and screaming to the Jeep. "Stop struggling!" he said.

"Let go of me!"

The woman was determined to drive him nuts. "Would you get in the damn Jeep, for Pete's sake? Can't you see it's storming?" As if to back up his claim, a gust of wind flattened her blouse against her.

"Ah, hell," Cutter said. Without warning, he bent down and swept her off her feet and carried her to the waiting vehicle. "Stop acting like a hysterical child," he yelled into her face a second before he slammed the door. He grabbed the dog and shoved him in back, then climbed in and started down the road once more.

Cutter parked in front of the Simmses' house a few minutes later. "Stay in your seat until I get the dog out," he told Ellie, who had remained surprisingly quiet. A minute later, he helped her out of the Jeep and led her toward the house. "Didn't you leave your porch light on?" he asked, noting how dark the place was as they tried to pick their way across the soggy yard.

"Yes." Her voice trembled.

"Damn power must be off." He got her as far as the porch. "Wait here, and I'll grab a flashlight from the Jeep."

Ellie realized she was shivering as she reached into her pocket for the key. In the dark, she groped for the keyhole. Cutter was back a moment later with the light. He took the key from her, stabbed it into the lock, and shoved the door open. "I want to be alone," Ellie told him when he followed her inside.

"That's just too bad," he muttered, slamming the door behind him. "I'm not leaving until I'm sure you're okay."

"I'm just fine," she snapped, then realized she was shivering.

"Do you have any candles?"

"How would I know?"

"Let's try the kitchen." Cutter prodded her in that direction. They searched through several drawers, then beneath the sink. Finally, he found what he was looking for. "There's only one holder here, so we'll have to share." He lit the candle and set it on the counter, then gazed at Ellie.

She was a mess, covered from head to toe with mud. "I'll run you a hot bath," he told her, leaving the room with his flashlight before she could object. "Where's your bathrobe?" he asked when he returned.

Ellie looked up and found him watching her with what looked to be a great deal of concern. "In the bedroom," she said. "Hanging on the back of the door." He nodded and hurried toward it. When he returned, he picked up the candle.

"Come on, the tub should be filled by now," he said, motioning for her to follow him.

Ellie was simply too tired to argue. Besides, a hot bath sounded like just the thing she needed. She stood and followed him into the next room where he set the candle on the side of the tub. "Can you manage now?" he asked. When she nodded, he closed the door.

Ellie sat there for a moment more as she listened to Cutter moving around in the kitchen. Finally she stripped off her wet clothes and sank into the tub of hot water. She leaned back and closed her eyes as a knock sounded on the door and she remembered she hadn't locked it.

"Ellie, where are your towels?" Cutter called back. "I've got to dry this dog off before he drowns in his own puddle."

"The towels are in here," Ellie said. "In the linen closet. If you'll give me a second—"

"Okay, I'm coming in."

"Cutter, wait!" She huddled into a tight ball in the tub.

"I won't look," he said, stepping inside the door and shining his light on the closet that held the linens. He opened the door, fumbled for an old towel, then disappeared on the other side again. "You okay in there?" he asked.

Ellie relaxed. "I'm fine."

There wasn't a drop of mud to be found anywhere on her when Ellie came out of the bathroom some time later, her hair freshly shampooed and falling damp at her shoulders. Cutter was in the kitchen drinking coffee. "How'd you manage that?" she asked, knowing the coffeemaker couldn't run without electricity.

He motioned toward the stove. "I found an old

stove-top coffeepot under the sink when I was looking for more candles. Have a seat and I'll pour you a cup."

Ellie took a seat at the table and waited for him to prepare her cup. "Cutter, I'm sorry I lost my temper back there," she said once he'd handed her the cup.

He offered her a weary smile. "And I'm sorry about the coon."

She raised her eyes to his and their gazes locked. "I have trouble with violence . . . and blood."

"I understand."

She shook her head. "I don't think you do." She paused and took a deep breath. "That man . . . the one who raped me. He used a knife."

Cutter closed his eyes. It tore his guts out to think of someone hurting her in any way. "He cut you?"

She could feel the tears burning the back of her eyes. "He stabbed me in the back. I'm okay now, but I spent some time in the hospital because of it."

The look on his face was one of horror and regret. He took the chair next to her and reached for her hand. "I'm sorry, Ellie. So sorry."

She sighed, and her eyes flooded with tears. "I thought by now I'd be over it. I've always been such a positive person. This experience really dragged me down. I'm not sure I'll ever be the same."

Cutter got out of his chair and knelt beside her, sliding his arms around her waist. He couldn't handle her tears, and he felt his heart constrict at the sight of them. "You probably won't ever be the same, Ellie," he said, "but that doesn't mean you have to give up living." He paused and struggled for a moment with his own emotions. "I never thought I could give a damn about anybody, but tonight I almost lost my mind when I couldn't find you. And then I saw you standing in the road, wet and crying, and all I could think of was making you better. I wish there was something I could do for you, Ellie. I wish I could take away the pain. I wish you never had to be afraid again."

Her bottom lip trembled. "Would you stay with me tonight?" she asked softly. "I don't want to be alone. I'm ashamed to admit it, but I'm still afraid of the dark." She gave a shudder. "I've spent enough time in the dark for one night."

"Yes, baby, I'll stay," he said, trying to comfort her in any way he could. "For as long as you need me."

She smiled as her eyes filled and the tears fell down her cheeks. "You know, you're not such a rogue after all."

This made him laugh. "Don't tell anyone. I wouldn't want to blow my image. I worked hard for it."

Ellie suddenly realized he was still wet. "You need a hot shower," she said. "I'm trying to think of something of mine you could wear."

"I'm sure I have something in the back of my Jeep," he told her. "Besides, I need to bring in that bag of dog food I promised you. If that mutt of yours gets any skinnier, he's going to dry up and blow away." He stood.

Ellie reached for his hand, hating to let him go for even a moment. "You really don't mind staying?"

His look was tender. "Not in the least." He hurried out into the rain for his belongings.

Eight

Ellie's heart lurched in her chest when a freshly showered Cutter walked into the kitchen wearing the same cutoffs he'd worn the day he had helped her plant her garden. One glimpse of his strong body made her pulse quicken.

"You're staring, Ellie."

A rush of color stained her cheeks. She coughed, then cleared her throat, pretending not to be affected by the sight of his powerful chest. Even standing across the room from him, she was aware of his strength and solidity. She knew without touching him that his flesh would be warm and tough as leather. "I'm sorry. I wasn't expecting . . ." She paused. What wasn't she expecting? To be so undeniably attracted to him?

"I know they aren't much to look at," he said, apologizing for his clothes, "but they're all I have at the moment."

"Would you like to borrow one of my T-shirts?" she asked.

He shook his head, then pondered it further.

113

"Unless it bothers you for me to walk around like this."

"No, I'm fine," she said a bit too quickly. But she wondered how she would be able to concentrate on anything else with that massive chest of his stealing all her attention. "Are you hungry?" she asked. "I've got peanut butter and jelly." She had already fed and watered Duke and found an old rug for him to sleep on at the front door.

"That sounds good." Cutter took a seat at the table and waited silently while she set out the ingredients they would need for sandwiches, then grabbed a bag of chips and two root beers. They ate their sandwiches with only the sound of the rain pelting against the windows to break the silence.

"You don't want the dog, do you?" she asked him after a moment, thinking she needed to say something.

He offered her a slight smile. "Why don't you give me a few days to think about it? Who knows, you might grow attached to him."

"I can't take him back to Savannah with me."

"We'll see."

She decided not to push him for the time being. "It doesn't sound like the rain is going to let up any time soon," Ellie said instead. "Does the power go out often?"

"All the time," he told her. "But they'll have it restored by morning."

"Morning?"

"I'll stay until it comes back on." He noticed how tired she looked. "Why don't you go to bed?" he suggested. "If you'll give me a blanket, I'll take the couch."

"You don't have to sleep on the couch when

there are three perfectly good bedrooms." She grabbed his flashlight as she rose from the table and hurried to the linen closet for fresh sheets. Cutter followed her into the middle bedroom and held the candle while she made up the bed. "I know it's childish of me to be afraid of the dark," she said, suddenly feeling very self-conscious with him. There was something vaguely sensuous about making the bed in which he was to sleep.

"Everybody's afraid of something."

She glanced up at him and saw that he was watching her intently. He radiated a vitality and strength that drew her to him like steel shavings to a magnet. She could feel the pull, subtle but sure. The very air around her seemed electrified. "Everybody except for you."

"You'd be surprised, Ellie."

She studied the lean, dark face. Even though his expression was closed, she sensed a vulnerability about him, a silent sadness. Did Cutter Beaumont have demons of his own? she wondered. She was suddenly more curious than ever about the man and his past, which she knew included an ex-wife. But her own experience had taught her not to probe into other people's lives, so she didn't ask. Once the bed was made, she stared at him. She couldn't deny the spark between them and the unwelcome surge of excitement that rippled through her every time their gazes met. She had deliberately tried to shut out any physical awareness of him, but she'd failed.

"I hope you'll be comfortable," she said.

Lord, but she was pretty in the soft light. Pretty, and more feminine than any woman he'd ever met. "I'll be fine."

"There's an extra toothbrush in the medicine cabinet."

"Thanks."

"Well . . ." She paused and met his black-eyed gaze once more. "You know where everything is. Just help yourself."

He resisted the urge to take her in his arms once more, knowing he would never be able to stop with just one kiss. "Go to bed, Ellie. You look dead on your feet."

"Good night, Cutter." She left the room and made her way to her own bedroom at the back of the house, climbed beneath the crisp sheets, and blew out her candle. A moment later she heard Cutter fumbling in the medicine cabinet, no doubt trying to find the spare toothbrush with his flashlight. The sound of running water comforted her. It was nice having a man around for a change.

She'd had the dream dozens of times, but it never failed to terrify her. The sound of footsteps in a dark parking lot. A flash of silver. Hand tight against her mouth; knife to her throat. She tried to scream but couldn't. Panic filled her throat and kept the sounds from coming out. And then she was driving, that same knife pressed against her rib cage. Leaving the city behind, the lights sparkling below like precious jewels. The patch of woods. All that rain. Begging for her life. A numbing pain.

This time when she opened her mouth to scream, the sounds filled her head.

"Ellie?"

"Please, God, help me. Oh, God!"

"Ellie, wake up, dammit!"

Another scream ripped from her throat as Ellie bolted upright in the bed. "Stop!" she said, as the shadow came closer. "Please, don't!"

"Ellie, it's me, Cutter." He shook her.

"Cutter?"

"You were having a bad dream."

Ellie strained to see him in the dark. "Cutter?"

"Where's the candle?"

She tried to think. "On the nightstand. There are matches. . . ."

Fumbling in the dark, Cutter lit a match and touched it to the wick of the candle. A soft glow fell on his trembling hands. He sat on the edge of the bed and put his hands on her shoulders. "What is it?"

Ellie drew her knees to her chest and hugged herself tightly. She was shivering, her teeth chattered like a squirrel chewing an acorn. "It seems so real. Every time I have it I think it's happening all over again."

Cutter knew without a doubt that she had been dreaming about her rape. "Do you have the dream often?"

She offered him a bleak, tight-lipped smile. "More often than I'd like to."

Cutter's own mouth was pressed into a grim line. At the same time, he looked sympathetic. He touched her arm, trying to comfort her in whatever way he could. "Do you want to tell me about it?"

"It's too awful to talk about." She realized she was crying. "I saw a therapist for a while and attended a few rape-counseling sessions, but nothing seemed to work, so I stopped."

"It's going to take time, Ellie, but the more you talk about it, the better you'll feel." When she didn't respond, he went on. "Would you rather I left you alone now?"

"No. I want you to stay." She looked up at him

pleadingly. "Would you just sit here and hold me for a moment?"

Cutter knew there wasn't anything he wouldn't do for her, but it wasn't going to be easy holding her next to his body with only that flimsy T-shirt covering her. "Sure, baby," he said at last. She scooted over, and he moved next to her, stretching out his long legs. He leaned against the headboard and opened his arms. "Come here."

Ellie hesitated only a moment before going to him. He was as comforting as a wool blanket in winter. She began to relax. Finally, exhaustion won out and she sagged against his powerful chest. "Thanks for being here tonight," she said as her eyelids fluttered closed.

Cutter wondered if she had any idea how good she felt in his arms. Her body was slender and strong, with curves in all the right places. Her hair smelled like baby shampoo. He closed his eyes and tried to think of something else, but his body was reacting to her nearness. He had never wanted a woman so badly in his life. If Ellie had any idea how much he wanted her, she would scramble from the bed and run as far away from him as she could. Finally, she stopped shaking. He hugged her. "Better?"

"Mmm." She snuggled closer, enjoying the scent of soap and male flesh. "Cutter?"

He liked the way she said his name. "Yeah?"

"I never thought I would be attracted to another man after" —she paused—"you know."

He held his breath. He didn't want to hear her tell him she was even remotely attracted to him. How could she expect him to lie on her bed with her in his arms and do nothing. "Go to sleep, Ellie," he whispered, pressing his lips against her forehead.

"I should probably have my head examined," she confessed, "but I feel safe with you. I mean, I know you're a rogue and a sweet-talker and womanizer and that nothing could come of this, but"—she sighed—"I've never been afraid of you."

Cutter gazed at the shadows playing on the walls as the candle flickered, and he knew that, while she might not be afraid of him, he was scared to death of her. It almost made him laugh. Cutter Beaumont, who'd been burned and betrayed and had promised himself never again to love, had somehow fallen head over heels for the woman beside him.

When Ellie opened her eyes it was morning. A gray light filled the room. Outside the old-fashioned plate-glass window the rain came down in a fine mist. The room was cool. Beside her, Cutter Beaumont was large and warm and solid as concrete. She gazed up at his sleeping face and studied it. Even in sleep he was handsome as the devil, his face kindled with a sort of passionate beauty. Still, it was a strong face. The square jaw below suggested a stubborn streak in him that made Ellie smile. His ink-black hair was unruly and startling against the crisp white pillowcase beneath his head. There were touches of humor around his mouth that only added to his sensuality.

Ellie snuggled against him, taking comfort in his warmth. She was touched that he had stayed with her through the night, that he'd cared enough to simply hold her when he'd known there would be no sexual exchange between them.

Suddenly, Cutter's eyes fluttered open. He offered Ellie a sleepy smile and tightened his arms around her. "G'morning."

"Hi." She glanced away, feeling strangely shy with him now that he was awake.

"Did you sleep okay?"

One hand curled against his chest, Ellie felt the vibrations of his voice, the rich timbre. It lulled her senses, soothed her. His voice had an infinitely compassionate tone to it, so different from the usual playful banter. Still, there was an underlying sensuality there that made the moment even more intimate and sent a ripple of awareness through her. "I slept fine," she said at last. "Thanks for staying."

"My pleasure."

She forced herself to look at him. "About last night."

"It's okay, Ellie," he said. "I don't think you're a coward for being afraid of the dark."

"Not that part. I'm talking about when I admitted that I was attracted to you."

His soft, deceptively calm voice prodded her on. "Yeah?" Inside, though, his heart hammered against his rib cage.

"I meant it."

He stared wordlessly at her. A faint light glimmered from the depths of his black eyes; yet, a look of uncertainty remained fixed on his face. Lightly, he toyed with a curl at her cheek as though he were trying to buy time until he'd absorbed the news. "Yeah?" he said at last.

Ellie reached out and clutched his hand. His fingers were warm and sturdy. Their gazes locked. Finally, she smiled. "Is that all you have to say?"

His expression turned serious. "Frankly, I don't know *what* to say."

She pondered it. "You could say the feeling was mutual. But only if you mean it."

"If I weren't attracted to you, I wouldn't be here right now," he told her. "I wouldn't have spent the past ten days thinking of you." He paused. "But I'm not sure I'm the man for you, Ellie. I can't see you without wanting to hold you. And I can't kiss you without wanting to make love. I get hard just standing in the same room with you."

"I'm glad."

He couldn't have looked more surprised. "You are?"

"I want you to make love to me just as much as you want it, Cutter." Her face reddened as she said it. "I realized it that day we planted the garden, but I was ashamed to admit it even to myself. I figured I must be terribly dysfunctional to want a man after"—she paused and took a deep breath—"you know."

Cutter knew it hadn't been easy for her to tell him what she had. He adjusted himself, lying on his side propped on one elbow so he could look at her as he spoke. "Listen, Ellie. That creep made you feel as though sex is something dirty and vile. It doesn't have to be."

"He used me like a piece of meat."

He cupped her cheek. "I know, baby. But that's not the way it's supposed to be. Which is why I would never force myself on you. Half the pleasure of making love is watching the other person's response. I don't want you to shrink away from me in horror when I make love to you. I want you to enjoy it. I want to experience your arousal. I want to feel you tremble beneath me."

"I want those things too."

Suddenly it felt to Cutter as though the earth had come to a standstill. All he could do was stare at the woman before him and wonder what he could have done or said to have changed her mind. He took a deep, shuddering breath. "Are you sure, Ellie? Because if you're not—"

"I want you to make love to me, Cutter. I don't want to spend the rest of my life alone." She saw the reluctance in his eyes. "I have to learn to trust again," she told him. "Don't you see? I don't expect you to love me or make a commitment. I won't put a leash on you. But you're the first man I've trusted in more than a year."

Somewhere along the line, Cutter had begun to feel uneasy about what she was asking. He pulled his arm from behind her and raised up, then raked his fingers through his black hair. "I don't know, Ellie. This is beginning to sound like some sort of experiment. What if I start making love to you and you hate it?"

"I'm prepared for that."

"Well, I'm not," he said, sounding angry for the first time. "I've walked around for more than a week now becoming aroused whenever I thought of you. Oh, don't look so shocked, for Pete's sake! We're adults here. If you want sex from me, you've got to be prepared to go all the way. I swear I won't hurt you, but I can't take this indecision." He pushed himself up and stood. "Maybe you should think this over carefully, Ellie. We don't have to rush into anything."

"I have thought it over, Cutter. I want to make love with you. Not tomorrow or the next day. Now."

Nine

Cutter felt as though someone had pulled the floor out from under him. "Now?" The uncertainty on his face mingled with disbelief. There was an almost subtle note of pleading in his voice when he went on. "Ellie, are you sure you know what you're doing?"

For once, she was surprisingly calm. The past year had not been easy. She had hit rock bottom emotionally, certain that she would never again have a normal relationship with a man. And then she'd met Cutter. Cutter, who'd made her trust him despite his bad-boy image. Cutter, the last person she would have expected to want in her bed and in her life. But now that she had decided she did indeed want him, she felt free, at peace with herself, as though a storm had passed through her and left only tranquility in its wake. "I'm sure," she said softly. "But first, I want you to pull the shades."

Still stunned, Cutter moved woodenly to the windows and pulled the shades, taking some of the morning light from the room. She obviously was more modest than most of the women he'd known. "Okay, Ellie," he said, measuring his words carefully. "The shades are drawn. Now what? You're calling the shots here." He knew he was incapable at the moment.

"I want you to hold me."

His eyes were hooded and as unreadable as a stone wall as he approached her. "That's easy enough," he said, but the grim set of his mouth told her it might not be so easy. He reclaimed his spot on the bed and held her stiffly. "How's that?"

"It would be better if you'd just try and relax," she told him. In spite of herself, she chuckled.

Cutter stared at her, then suddenly threw back his head and let out a peal of laughter. "I don't believe this," he said. "How did I end up being the nervous one here?"

His own laugh was infectious, and she joined in until they were both laughing so hard, they couldn't stop. Just as they were about to get serious, Ellie hiccuped loudly, and it started all over again until she was wiping tears from her eyes. She fell against him weakly, holding her stomach where the poor muscles protested from too much laughter. "Stop!" she cried, playfully pounding her fists against his chest. And then, much to her surprise, she realized she was sprawled across him on the bed. All at once, their smiles vanished.

"Oh, Ellie." His voice was oddly gentle. He raised one of her fists to his face, pried it open with his thumb, and pressed his lips against her open palm. His breath was warm and moist on her skin, even as he kissed a path to her wrist. His movements were slow and seductive as his gaze traveled over her face and searched for signs of nervousness. There were none. With powerful hands, he reached for her and pulled her on top of him. Ellie sucked her breath in sharply when her thigh brushed against his hardness. Her thick lashes flew up in surprise.

He looked amused. "What'd you expect, Ellie?"

Apprehension flickered in her eyes and gnawed at her self-confidence. She was, at once, thrilled and frightened. "I'm not sure."

Letting her go, he cupped her face between powerful hands and regarded her. His gaze was compassionate and soft as a caress. "It's okay. I wouldn't hurt you for anything."

"I know."

Finally, he drew her head down and touched her lips lightly with his—once, twice, and again, reacquainting himself with the taste of her. Her soft curves molded to his lean body, fitting together like erotic puzzle pieces. He put his arms around her, resting them at the small of her back. Ellie sank against him and buried her face against his corded neck.

Cutter was touched to the core by the simple, almost girlish gesture. For a moment he simply held her, listened to her breathing, and wondered what he'd done to deserve having her appear so suddenly in his life. He wound a hand in her thick hair and lifted her head so that she was forced to look at him. The passion and the need he saw there took his breath away. He captured her mouth hungrily, then gently, but firmly rolled her off of him and eased her down onto her back.

The touch of his lips on hers sent a shockwave of emotion and desire through Ellie's body. She felt transported; her senses reeled as though the brain cells in her head had somehow short-circuited. She clung to him, as shocked as she was surprised by the way her body responded to his. She wanted Cutter Beaumont as she had never wanted another man before.

Slowly, seductively, he outlined her shape with his wide hands before skimming her bare thighs beneath the long T-shirt. He broke the kiss. "Okay?" he asked, then recaptured her lips when she nodded. And then, as gently as he could, he stroked her inner thigh. Ellie arched against him instinctively, desire flooding her body at his touch. Raising himself on elbows, Cutter freed her of the T-shirt, unable to wait another moment to see her. His gaze caressed her breasts.

"You're so pretty, Ellie," he said, his voice taking on a new huskiness. He stroked each breast and watched in fascination as her nipples became tight little buds. He covered one with his mouth. All the while, his hands never stilled, though he told himself over and over to slow down, take his time. He was greedy where she was concerned. He wanted all of her and more. Finally, he slipped his hand inside her panties. He held his breath. She opened herself to him, and he dipped his fingers inside. She was wet. His ears roared.

"Oh, Ellie," he whispered against her parted lips. "You do the nicest things."

And then it seemed as if they could not get their clothes off fast enough. Ellie's panties and his cutoffs were tossed aside as carelessly as last week's newspapers. Cutter explored her with his eyes and fingers, seeking out each hidden niche. Ellie did the same, taking pleasure in his large, hair-roughened body and taut muscles. She was no longer anxious. Her desire for him overrode any negative feelings she had. Her body ached and vibrated with the sexual desire she had thought long dead.

At last, Cutter swept her legs apart. He paused, his gaze locking with hers briefly before he entered her. She rose to meet him, her eager response matching his own. He was big and hard and hot, filling her to completion. She met each thrust, rocking with him until the old bed creaked and groaned beneath their weight and added sexy background music to their raspy breathing. She yielded to the need that had been building up for months beneath her fear, abandoned herself to the passion she'd never known with another man. She let go. Desire racked her body like liquid fire; a moan filled her throat and slipped from her lips. Cutter caught it with a kiss. Her thoughts split and became tiny fragments as she soared over the edge.

Cutter heard her cry out and knew he was a dead man. She was too hot, too tight. Her muscles contracted with orgasm, milking him until all control was lost. He thrust deeply into her, losing himself in her moist softness. Nothing else mattered. With a sigh of pleasure, he emptied himself inside of her and shuddered.

For a long time afterward, neither of them said anything. They lay there, eyes closed, arms and legs tangled, enjoying the moment. Finally, Ellie raised up. "Where are my clothes?" she said.

Feeling tired and as satisfied as a bullterrier with a ham bone, Cutter stretched and opened his eyes slowly. "You don't need clothes," he said, then reached for her. The amused look left his eyes the moment his hand made contact with her shoulder blade. "What the hell?"

Ellie sensed the change in him even before he

spoke. She snapped her head around and saw that he was staring at her back and the ugly scarring. In a matter of seconds his look had changed from sleepy contentment to horror and raw contempt. "I know it's not pretty," she said, glancing away in sudden embarrassment. "That's why I asked you to pull the shades."

"That's where he stabbed you?"

She looked at him. "Yes."

"Son of a bitch." Cutter sat up slowly, swung his legs over the side of the bed, and sat there. He couldn't even bear to look at her for a moment. "How long ago did it happen, Ellie?"

"Thirteen months, two weeks, and three days."

"You said you were in the hospital?"

"Yes, for a couple of weeks."

"Did you know him?"

"I'd never seen him before in my life."

He looked at her. "You have to tell me what happened. I have to know."

Ellie saw that he was trembling. Raw hurt glittered in his dark eyes. "It's not easy to talk about."

"Just tell me what you can."

Ellie studied him more closely. "Why do you want to know, Cutter? Why is it so important for you to hear the sordid details?"

He didn't answer right away. Finally, he sighed and raked his hands through his hair. "Because I think I'm falling in love with you, Ellie."

Ellie poured two cups of coffee and set them on the round table, then joined Cutter, who had remained quiet while she'd made the coffee, using the automatic coffeemaker now that power had been restored. She had promised to tell him everything once she'd had her first cup. She looked at him. "Okay, what do you want to know?" she asked at last.

His lips were pressed into a grim line. "Everything."

Ellie took a deep breath. Part of the problem of telling him about the rape, she realized, was the fear that his feelings for her would change. He had told her he thought he was falling in love with her, but she wouldn't even let herself accept that fact, when there was still so much he didn't know. She had to tell him, though. "It happened when I was leaving work late one night. We were getting ready for a large convention, and the hotel was short on staff. I was one of the last people to leave." She paused. "It was close to midnight when I went out to my car. I stuck the key in the lock and the next thing I knew someone was holding a knife at my throat."

She sounded like a mechanical doll, Cutter realized, all emotion gone from her voice. He wondered if it was because she had simply told the story so many times she knew it by heart, or if she was somehow able to detach herself emotionally when she was forced to repeat it. "What'd you do?"

"Well, once I got past the initial shock, I just tried to remain calm and follow his instructions. He told me he would kill me right there in the parking lot if I screamed. I knew he meant it."

"And then what?"

"He had me drive to a remote area. He kept the knife pressed against my rib cage." She was thoughtful for a moment. "Now that I look back, I keep thinking it would have been better if I'd rammed my car into someone else's or even jumped out of it while it was moving. There's a dozen things I could have done to escape, but—"

"But what?"

The wooden expression on her face crumbled. Tears filled her eyes. "I was too scared to think. Petrified. And he kept promising he wouldn't hurt me if I did as he said. I thought maybe he was running from the police and just needed a ride out of town." She shook her head. "It wasn't until he told me to stop the car on that dirt road that I realized he intended to rape me." The tears slid down her cheeks. "He told me he'd been watching me for a while. He told me—" A sob caught in her throat. "Some of it's too disgusting to repeat."

Cutter reached for her hand. "Tell me the rest, Ellie. I have to know."

She shook her head. Why did he have to know? What was the point? So that he could be reminded of her humiliation and degradation every time he held her? "What's to tell?" she said. "He raped me. I think because he was so nervous he had trouble . . . you know."

Cutter nodded.

"He told me to talk dirty to him. I didn't know what to say. He slapped me around until I could think of something. I told him all the sleazy things I thought he wanted to hear. I told him things—" She paused as another sob escaped her lips. "Oh, God, it was awful!"

Cutter pulled her onto his lap. He had never known such anger in his life, such intense hatred. He had never killed a man, although he'd come close once, then decided the creep wasn't worth going to prison over. But he knew, deep in his heart, he would gladly kill the man who'd done this to Ellie, even if it meant spending his life in a roach-infested cell. But that's not what Ellie needed to hear from him at that moment. "It's okay, baby," he said at last, and pressed a kiss against her forehead. "You did what you had to do."

Ellie wasn't convinced. "You don't understand. The things he did to me. The things he made me do to him. And the whole time it was going on, I begged him not to hurt me. I thought if I just cooperated, he wouldn't kill me. I can't believe I was so stupid."

"What do you mean?"

"Because he didn't try to disguise himself. I had seen him, and he knew I could identify him. Don't you see? I should have known then and there that he planned to kill me."

"So when it was over he stabbed you?" Cutter realized his own voice had taken on a mechanical quality. Perhaps he needed to remain at least partially detached. Otherwise, he would just fly into a rage, and he wouldn't be worth a damn to her.

"He stabbed me three times," she said. "The first two times, I cried and pleaded for my life. After the third time, I decided to play dead. He seemed convinced that he'd really killed me. He climbed into my car and drove away."

"What did you do?"

"I barely had enough strength to even raise my head, but I knew if I didn't try to find my way back to the road I'd bleed to death. Still, it was way out in the boonies, so I didn't even know if anybody would be driving out there that time of night. But I crawled out to the middle and waited. I must have lost consciousness. When I woke up I was in the hospital."

"Who found you?"

"A teenage couple. From what I understand, they'd been out parking. The boy said he almost ran over me."

Cutter continued to hold her for a moment. "So you stayed in the hospital for two weeks?"

She nodded. "There was a nice, middle-aged woman who provided rape counseling. She was with me every day. I don't know how I would have made it without her. Then I started seeing a therapist, and I just tried to put my life back together. But I was scared it would happen to me again, so I took a couple of self-defense classes. I'm not sure whether it helped or not." Fresh tears blurred her vision. "At first, I just wished—"

"What do you wish?" he asked gently.

"I wished he would have finished me off."

"How can you say that, Ellie?"

Her voice trembled. "I thought death would have been easier than having to deal with it every day of my life. Every time I close my eyes I replay the scene in my mind of what I should have done."

"What do you think you should have done?"

"I should have tried to escape. I should have fought back. Most women would have fought back."

"You don't know that."

"I had nothing to lose by fighting back," she told him. "He tried to kill me anyway. At least I wouldn't have to live with the terrible memories. And the knowledge that I'm a coward."

Cutter looked at her. "I don't think you're a coward, Ellie. Look what you did. Even though you were bleeding to death, you crawled through the woods and to the road to save your life." He paused. "But none of that really matters now, does it?" At her perplexed look, he went on. "It's in the past, Ellie. The real test of bravery comes now. Are you prepared to put that experience behind you and go on with your life?"

She thought about it. "Believe me, nothing would make me happier than to leave it behind. Unfortunately, it's not so easy. I still have trouble trusting people, strangers especially. I used to be outgoing. I used to love people. Now I'm suspicious of them."

"Were you suspicious of me?"

"Maybe just a little. But I decided you had to have a few scruples to be elected sheriff and mayor." She smiled. "And I figured you'd prefer charming the pants off a woman to forcing her."

He grinned and tightened his arms around her waist. "Well, you got that right. I want my women to cry out in ecstasy, not fear." He gazed into her eyes a moment, then kissed her lightly. "So where does this leave us?"

"I'm not sure. I'm only going to be here a few weeks, then I have to go back to work. You realize that the last thing on my mind was to get involved with a man while I was here. I planned to use this time to sort of come to terms with what happened and try to get over it."

"Why did you feel you had to leave Savannah for that?"

"Everybody in my family tries to pretend it never happened," she said. "So do friends and coworkers. And, as you know, it isn't easy for me to talk about it. I kept thinking if I just pushed it aside, it would eventually go away, but that didn't happen. The nightmares only got worse."

"Is there anything I can do?"

"Just being here and knowing I can count on

you to understand why I act the way I do helps more than you know." Her eyes clouded. "Seeing that coon die last night really sent me over the edge."

"I'm sorry you had to go through that," he said, his tone compassionate. "I didn't get a kick out of it myself."

She was quiet for a moment. Reflectively, she went on. "I think I'm doing better than I was in the beginning," she said optimistically. "For a long time I would break out into a cold sweat if somebody stood too close to me in the supermarket line or brushed by me in the hall at work. I couldn't stand physical contact of any kind. I certainly never thought I would be able to"—she paused— "you know."

She saw that his cup was empty, and she carried it to the coffeemaker and refilled it. The rain had slowed into a steady drizzle. "So what are your plans for the day?" she asked, thinking it was time they talk about something else.

Cutter knew it was her way of changing the subject, and he decided to go along with it instead of questioning her further. She'd been through enough for one morning. He reached out, grabbed her around the waist, and pulled her back into his lap. She shrieked playfully but went to him without protest. He kissed her long and hard.

Finally, he broke the kiss. "Well, as much as I hate to do it, I need to get home and dress for work."

Ellie saw that it wasn't quite eight o'clock. "Isn't it a little early to open the saloon?"

He shook his head. "Clarence and I have an office in back. In fact, that's where he sleeps most nights. I go in early to take care of my sheriff's duties, what there is of them, then open the saloon for lunch." He grinned. "It's the only place on the island where folks can buy my famous suicide chili dogs and garlic pickles. It's also the town meeting place."

"So I've gathered," she told him. "Doesn't it get to be too much on you, trying to run a store and a saloon and act as sheriff, all at the same time?"

"Not when you assign other people to do the work," he said with a laugh. "Which reminds me. I have someone coming in around five to run the saloon tonight. I was sort of hoping you and I could go out."

"Go out?"

"Yeah, like on a date."

"Where on earth would we go?"

"We're not glued to this island, Ellie. I was thinking I might take you to a fancy restaurant on the mainland. We can take the ferry over. What do you say?"

Ellie felt a little nervous at the thought of leaving Erskine, although she couldn't figure out why. "I don't know, Cutter. Wouldn't we have just as much fun if we stayed here? I could try to cook something."

He saw that she was truly anxious about the prospect of going. "Look, Ellie, as much as I love this island, even *I* have to get off of it once in a while and go out to eat or catch a movie. Come on, you'll have a great time. I know just the place."

"Okay," she said after a minute, fixing a bright smile to her face. "Anything is better than having to eat my cooking."

Ten

Ellie let Duke out as soon as Cutter pulled away in his Jeep, then she carried fresh food and water to the back porch so the animal could eat. She was surprised to find Franklin D. sitting on the steps, one arm slung across the dog's back.

"Franklin D., what a surprise," she said. "Did you come by to visit your old friend Duke?" When the boy looked puzzled, she hurried on. "I changed his name," she said. "I couldn't very well stick him with the name Ugly." Franklin D. nodded as though it made perfect sense.

Ellie joined the boy on the steps and they watched Duke eat as though he hadn't had a meal in weeks. They laughed. "I think I should have named him Porky Pig," Ellie said, "because he eats like a pig." The boy's expression softened after a moment and became wistful. "You miss him, don't you?"

He nodded.

She felt sorry for the boy. She suspected he didn't have many friends. "Do you think your daddy would change his mind about letting you keep him?"

This time Franklin D. shook his head, giving her an emphatic no.

"Okay, tell you what. If you'll help me take care of Duke until I find him a good home, you can visit as often as you like. Maybe you could even feed him for me." The boy nodded enthusiastically. She hoped she wouldn't make it harder on the boy by allowing him to grow more attached to the animal. "First, though, we have to find him a place to sleep."

Ellie decided the best place would be the back porch where the washing machine sat. It would offer shelter from the rain. She propped the screen door open with a brick so Duke could go in and out, then retrieved the old rug from the front porch for him. She also showed Franklin how much food and water to put in the bowls and stored the bag of dry food in the closet-size storage area off to one side so that Franklin D. could get to it by himself if he needed to. "You can fill the water bowl using the spigot out back," she told him, "and I think we need to feed him both in the morning and late afternoon."

Franklin D. nodded.

"Now, why don't I make breakfast for us," she said, and ushered the boy inside. "You can wash up in the bathroom," she told him, then poured them each a glass of juice while he did so. She wished that she had offered to make breakfast for Cutter while he was there, then decided it might be better to wait awhile before she proved what an awful cook she really was. She smiled just thinking of how they'd spent the morning, how kind he'd been the night before. She missed him already. "Do you like scrambled eggs?" she asked Franklin D. when he returned, his hands and face freshly scrubbed.

He nodded.

"Good, because that's about the only thing I can cook without burning it to smithereens." He grinned, and she handed him a loaf of bread. "Why don't you toast the bread while I do the eggs?"

Ellie kept the conversation going while they prepared their simple breakfast. The boy responded to each of her comments with a small grunt or nod. "One day I'm going to teach you to say my name," she told him once they sat down to their meal. "Would you like that?" His eyes clouded. "It's not difficult to say it, you know. It's like taking two letters from the alphabet, L and E, and putting them together. Do you think you could say my name, Franklin D.?"

He shook his head, then turned his attention to his breakfast.

Ellie decided not to push. Instead, she scooped up some of the scrambled eggs onto her fork and tasted. "Not bad for a woman who has spent her lifetime avoiding the kitchen, huh?"

Franklin D. grinned again.

They were in the process of clearing away the dishes when someone knocked on the back door. Peeking through the window, Ellie saw Rose Wilcox standing outside. "It's your mother," she told the boy, then hurried to the back porch to let her in.

"Have you seen Franklin D.?" Rose asked, her eyes wide with concern. "I went into his room to wake him up this morning and he was gone. I've searched everywhere."

"He's here," Ellie told her, and watched her expression turn to relief, then anger. "Didn't he tell you he was coming over here?" she asked, holding the door for her to pass through.

"No, he didn't." Rose stalked into the house where she found Franklin D. standing at the sink rinsing his plate. "Just who do you think you are, leaving the house and coming out here without my permission?" she demanded, hands on hips. "And didn't I tell you not to pester Miss Parks?"

"He wasn't bothering me," Ellie cut in quickly. "I think he just missed the dog."

Rose regarded her. "Don't tell me you let Booker T. talk you into taking that scrawny animal," she said in a voice that suggested she thought Ellie had more sense.

Ellie blushed. "Well, I sort of agreed to look after him until I found a good home for him."

"Ain't nobody goin' to want that dog. He's too ugly." As if noticing Franklin D.'s plate for the first time, Rose went on. "And don't tell me you made Miss Parks feed you too!"

"I invited Franklin D. to have breakfast with me," Ellie said. "It gets lonely eating by myself all the time. I hope it's okay."

Rose seemed to ponder it. "Just don't let him make a nuisance of himself," she said, then turned to her son. "As for you, young man, you don't *ever* leave the house without my permission. I won't let you off so easy next time."

The boy nodded solemnly.

"Rose, let me pour you a cup of coffee," Ellie offered.

The other woman hesitated only a moment before accepting. "I reckon one cup won't hurt. I didn't mean to come in making such a ruckus, but

I don't like not knowing where my children are. I automatically think the worse."

Ellie knew without being told that it had to do with losing a son to a drowning accident. She touched the woman's shoulder lightly. "I'm sorry, Rose. I didn't think to ask Franklin D. if he had your permission to be here." The woman's eyes filled with tears. Ellie turned to the boy, who looked ashamed for what he'd done. "Why don't you check on Duke for me while I visit with your mother?" Ellie waited for him to go. "Are you okay, Rose?" she asked softly.

"You know what happened to my oldest boy, don't you?" When Ellie nodded she went on. "It's hard living with it sometimes," Rose said. "I still have bad days."

Ellie took her hand and squeezed it. "I understand."

Once Ellie saw that Rose was going to be okay, she poured them each a cup of coffee. "Rose, I was wondering," she began hesitantly, not wanting to upset the woman further but feeling it was important. "Does Franklin D. ever say anything?"

The woman's eyes clouded over, and she looked embarrassed that Ellie had brought it up. "No."

Ellie leaned closer. "I don't mean to pry, Rose, but why don't you get him some help?"

Rose answered matter-of-factly. "I figure Franklin D. will talk when he's good 'n' ready and not a moment before." She paused. "Besides, we can't afford to take him to one of those fancy psychiatrists, if that's what you're suggestin'. Do you have any idea what they charge these days?"

"You could go to the county mental health center. They would only charge what you're capable of paying."

"That ain't the only problem. Franklin D. is terrified of the water. He'd rather take a beatin' than set foot on a boat."

"What will you do when it's time for him to go to school?"

"I reckon I'll have to teach him at home. My husband and I both been through the tenth grade. We can at least get him that far."

"Yes, but that's not the same thing. Franklin D. needs to meet other children his age. You, yourself, told me how badly you wanted your children to get off this island. If he doesn't get a good education, he'll never find a decent job."

Rose took a sip of her coffee, then shoved her cup aside and stood. "Look, Ellie, I know you mean well, but you best let me and my husband worry about Franklin D. He'll be okay."

Ellie smiled. "In other words, you want me to mind my own business."

Rose chuckled. "Somethin' like that, yes." She walked to the door and pushed it open, then glanced over her shoulder once. "Seems to me you got enough to worry about."

"What do you mean?"

"Someone told me they saw Cutter Beaumont's Jeep in your driveway in the wee hours of the morning. You're going to have your hands full with that man." She grinned. "And stop looking so embarrassed. We both knew it was bound to happen sooner or later."

Cutter surprised Ellie at lunch by showing up with a bag of his famous suicide chili dogs, two fat garlic pickles, and a bag of salt-and-vinegar potato chips. Ellie couldn't help but feel a bit shy with him after the way they'd spent the morning. Still, she was glad to see him and she wished, for once, she'd taken a little more time on her hair. For more than a year she hadn't cared how she looked. Her eyes stung as she unpacked the bag. "I don't know if we should eat this stuff or hang it on the back porch to keep evil spirits away."

Cutter slipped his arms around her waist. "I been thinking about you all morning. Did you miss me?"

She didn't quite know how to respond to him or his nearness, and she was almost relieved when he released her. She was out of practice where the opposite sex was concerned. It had been simpler when she had thought of him as simply Cutter Beaumont, the insensitive flirt. Now that she had seen another side to him she was confused as to what to think. Finally, she nodded. "I spent the morning with Franklin D. Rose stopped in for coffee after that."

"Rose is a good woman. She and her husband have lived on the island all their lives."

"Well, she is probably irritated with me at the moment. I questioned her about taking Franklin D. to a doctor."

He chuckled and tweaked her nose. "Couldn't keep quiet, could you?"

"I think somebody should do something, Cutter. I'm surprised *you* haven't."

"Listen, Ellie, I learned a long time ago not to mess with these people when it comes to their customs and beliefs and the way they do things. They're different from what you're used to." When she didn't look convinced, he went on. "Sure, they all attend the Baptist church on Sunday, but most of them practice a little voodoo here and there as well." He paused at the skeptical look she shot him. "I'm serious. Haven't you ever noticed how many people around here paint the frames around their windows blue? That's to keep the evil spirits out. They still use charms and herbs for healing. Franklin D. walked around with garlic and roots hanging around his neck for the first six months after the accident. His parents probably figure if that won't heal him, nothing will."

"This isn't the Stone Age, Cutter, this is the nineties."

"Well, you aren't going to convince anyone around that a shrink would be able to help the boy. They'll laugh you right off this island." He put his arms around her once more. "Now, let's talk about where we want to go tonight."

Ellie started getting ready for her date with Cutter at two o'clock that afternoon, knowing he planned to pick her up at five-thirty and drive to the main dock for the six o'clock ferry. Looking at herself in the bathroom mirror, she saw that she had indeed neglected herself over the past year. Her hair was dry as hay and not without its share of split ends. Well, she couldn't do anything about the split ends at the moment, but she could at least use a conditioner on her poor, limp mane. She checked her makeup and toiletry case and found what she needed for a hot oil treatment as well as a conditioning pack. Finally, with her hair greased and wrapped in a towel and her face smeared with cream, she stepped into a hot bath laced with baby oil.

Lord, she had forgotten what it was like to pamper herself. Ellie leaned back in the massive claw-foot tub and closed her eyes. Twice the water grew cold and she had to warm it up. Finally, at three o'clock, she rinsed both hair and body and stepped out of the tub. She dried briskly, then lotioned herself from head to toe. Next came the badly needed pedicure and manicure. Sitting in front of an open window, she let her hair dry naturally, curling around her face in a flattering style.

Ellie frowned when she picked up her makeup tools. She had not done a whole lot with makeup over the past year, taking a very Spartan attitude toward it. It did not take a genius to figure out why; she didn't want to look good for any man.

"Rape has absolutely nothing to do with the way you look, Ellie," Dr. Brenner had told her in the very first session. "It's a control thing. Why do you think old women and babies are raped?"

Of course, logically, Ellie knew all that. Emotionally, though, she hadn't been willing to take the chance. But now, as she gazed at the young woman in the mirror, she realized she couldn't continue to neglect herself and deny herself clothes and makeup simply because she was afraid of being raped again. She now had the tools to protect herself.

Ellie had not realized she'd put on weight until she stepped inside her dress, a black-and-white raw silk polka-dot dress she had packed on a whim, then stuffed in the back of her closet because she hadn't figured on wearing it while she was on the island. The last time she'd worn it the dress had hung on her as badly as an old sheet. Now it was snug on her hips and fell into a graceful tulip hemline at her knees.

Standing at the full-length mirror that hung on

the back of the bedroom door, Ellie wondered if she had overdone it with the makeup, and she suppressed the notion to tear the dress off and scrub her face. She was still struggling with doubts when Cutter knocked on her front door a few minutes later.

His eyes almost popped out of his head when he saw her. The Ellie he'd gotten to know over the past weeks was pretty, but the woman standing before him now was a knockout. He let out a low whistle of approval as he studied her. "Whoa, mama!"

She blushed. "Is that good or bad?"

"Definitely good."

Ellie took a moment to study him as well, from his charcoal pleated trousers to the dress shirt and lightweight blazer. "You shaved," she said, noting the absence of stubble on his jaw.

Cutter looked slightly embarrassed. "Yeah, well, I pick up the old razor every once in a while just to make sure I still know how to use it. You ready to go?"

She nodded. "Just let me grab my purse and lock up," she said, disappearing inside once more while Cutter waited on the front steps. As Cutter led her to his Jeep, she glanced up and saw Franklin D. crossing her front yard.

Ellie waved and smiled at the boy and he smiled back. "Are you here to feed Duke?" she asked.

He nodded.

"Well, you know where to find his food," she said. "He's on the back porch napping, so he'll be glad to see you." The boy glanced from her to Cutter and back to her again. "Mr. Beaumont and I are going to the mainland for dinner." She noticed her words had drawn a frown from the boy, and she went to him, kneeling before him. "It's okay, Franklin D.," she said, remembering his mother had told her how the boy feared the water and the ferryboats. "I'll be here when you come to feed Duke in the morning. Maybe you can have breakfast with me again." After a moment, he offered her a slight smile. "May I have a hug?" she asked. He responded by throwing his thin arms around her neck, and Ellie was almost moved to tears. "Tell you what," she whispered. "If you're good, I'll bring you a present. How's that?"

He nodded excitedly, hugged her once more, then hurried to the back of the house in search of Duke.

Standing at the Jeep, Cutter had watched the exchange between Ellie and Franklin D. He was touched to the core by what he saw, and it struck him as odd that two people who were so different could have become such fast friends. Then he realized it was not at all strange. Ellie and Franklin D. had both suffered and were trying to come to terms with it. He offered her a gentle smile as she hurried to the Jeep.

Cutter exchanged a word of greeting with the old captain when he and Ellie stepped onto the rumbling ferryboat a little later, then led Ellie toward the front, keeping a protective hand at her back. They stood at the railing as the sputtering contraption made its way across the bay to the mainland. Cutter noticed the anxious look drawing Ellie's brows together.

"I know it sounds like something Fred Flintstone would travel on," he said, indicating the boat, "but, other than being slow, it's very safe."

"What would you do if you had to cross the bay

quickly?" she asked. "Say, if someone needed a doctor fast?"

Cutter leaned against the railing. "Clarence Davis and I have both been trained in first aid and CPR," he told her. "But in the event of a serious emergency, the hospital would send their helicopter over. It has only happened twice since I've lived here. Once, when Meekin Brady gave birth to twins in my saloon, and"—he paused—"when Franklin D.'s brother drowned."

"Who pulled him out of the water?"

Cutter hesitated, then met her curious gaze. "I did. Clarence and I both worked with the boy until the paramedics arrived, but it was too late."

"How come nobody saw him go in?"

"It happened the first of January. It was cold as blazes that day. Nobody was out fishing on the docks except Franklin D. and his brother, who was still out of school for the Christmas holidays. The ferry had just come through, so the whole area was empty. Clarence and I were making rounds when the boy came running up to the Jeep with this wild look in his eyes, yelling that his brother had fallen off the pier and hadn't come back up." Cutter glanced away from her. "The kid fell and struck his head on a rock and drowned in about three feet of water."

Ellie shook her head sadly. "And Franklin D. stopped talking," she said.

Cutter sighed. "They kept him and his mother sedated for a couple of days. Rose took it real hard. I think that's probably one of the reasons she wasn't concerned about Franklin D.'s silence at first. She was having a hard enough time dealing with the tragedy. She wouldn't even let the preacher visit at first. She's better now."

Ellie gazed across the water where dark clouds scuttled across the horizon. "That's so sad," she said after a moment.

Cutter took her hand. "Yeah, it's sad, Ellie, but life goes on, and we have to make the best of it. If we sit and brood over all the bad things that go on in this world, we wouldn't have time to enjoy the good things."

"Are you speaking from experience?"

He shrugged. "Everybody has ups and downs, Ellie." He looked at her. "Now, before we go on to a happier topic and discuss what we're going to eat for dinner, I want you to answer a question for me. And be completely honest," he added in a tone that suggested her answer meant a lot to him.

She arched both brows, wondering what it could possibly be. "Okay," she said. "Ask me."

"Do you think I resemble Don Johnson on *Miami Vice*?"

Eleven

The restaurant had a casual elegance about it that reminded Ellie of those on the Savannah waterfront. Once she and Cutter were seated next to a window facing the bay, he asked for a wine menu and, after a brief discussion with the maître d', ordered what Ellie considered to be an excellent vintage.

"How do you know so much about wine?" she asked him when the man hurried away.

He shrugged. "I'm a saloon owner. I make it my business to know."

"Yes, but you don't carry expensive wines in the Last Chance."

He looked amused. "Is this an inquisition?"

"Of course not. But you know everything there is to know about me. At least the important things."

He saw that she wasn't about to give up. "Okay, okay," he said, raising both hands in surrender. "I used to be in a line of work that required that I travel a lot and entertain big shots who liked good wine. Satisfied?"

"What kind of work?"

"Selling helicopter parts. It was my job to schmooze purchasing people."

She smiled. "And were you a good schmoozer?"

"The best."

"So how come you're not still doing it?"

Cutter was prevented from answering right away when the maître d' returned with their bottle of wine. He was glad to have a moment to gather his thoughts, half hoping he could change the subject on Ellie and go on to something else.

"Well?" she said the moment their wine was poured and they were alone again.

"Ellie, there are a few things you don't know about me," he said after a moment.

"That doesn't surprise me. I thought I was a closed person, but I'm beginning to think I've met my match."

He offered her a tight smile. "Well, like I told you before, when I was in the army, a friend and I worked on helicopters and designed a much-needed part. We were successful."

"How successful?"

"We became overnight millionaires."

"I'm impressed."

"Don't be. It only lasted a few short years." He paused in reflection. "Funny how many friends you have when you're rich. I must've gotten better looking, too, because I had women all over me."

"That's the part I *don't* want to hear," she told him.

"Yes, well, I ended up marrying one of them. A rich Texas socialite. It was not a successful union."

"What happened?"

"She was spoiled and used to having her own

way, and I simply didn't give a damn. It was as much my fault as hers. Anyway, I was testing a helicopter one day, and I went down. Crashed and burned, as they say."

Ellie heard her own gasp. "And you didn't die?"

"I jumped out before it hit the ground and exploded." He offered her a sheepish grin. "And almost broke every bone in my body doing it."

"Oh, how awful!"

"They had me pegged for a goner. I didn't come out of the coma for weeks. When I finally woke up, I found myself in a body cast, and that's exactly where I spent the next few months of my life."

"Okay, let's go back to the wife part," she said, at the moment more curious about the woman he'd married.

"Oh, that." His expression turned sour. "Well, little did I know she and my partner were having an affair. When I didn't come out of the coma and it looked as if I was going to die, they took every last dime out of the company and moved to the Virgin Islands. I had no choice but to file bankruptcy, and my lawyer threw in the divorce for half price."

"That must've been hard for you."

"Yeah, I could have used the money."

She frowned. "I meant losing your wife."

He shrugged. "Actually, he did me a favor by taking her off my hands. But it really burned me about losing the company. As soon as I got on my feet, I went looking for them. I'd promised myself I was going to kill him with my bare hands. I almost did."

Ellie took a sip of her wine. The look in his eyes was startling. She realized she was seeing the brutal side of Cutter Beaumont. She had suspected it was there all along, lying just below the surface. He would make a wonderful friend and lover, but an awesome enemy. "So then you moved to Erskine?"

He nodded. "I wanted to get as far from civilization as I could. I suppose you might say I was bitter at the time. I scraped enough money together to open my saloon, and the rest, as they say, is history."

She pondered all he'd told her. She would, of course, like to know more about the ex-wife, but she figured she would have to get a little out of him at a time. "So it seems we both came to Erskine to escape the past."

"I did at first, but that was a long time ago. I stayed here because I liked it. But I don't have to hide because I didn't do anything wrong, and neither did you."

"Some people still feel women who are raped were somehow asking for it."

"That's crap, and you know it."

"Some husbands can't handle their wives being raped. I know of cases where it has destroyed the marriage."

"Perhaps there wasn't much of a marriage to begin with," he said. He leaned closer. "Look, if you're asking me if I have a problem making love to you because of it, the answer is no. I just think it's a shame they never caught the guy. Are the police still looking for him?"

She shrugged. "As far as I know. But there's not as much activity on the case. When I first got out of the hospital, it seemed I was going back and forth to the police station a lot, looking at mug shots and lineups. As time went on, they stopped calling me." She sighed. "At this point, I'd rather they just leave me alone."

"You want to catch the guy, don't you?"

"Yes, of course. But I'm ready to put this all behind me now and go on with my life." She stared down at her wineglass. "There are other reasons, though. I don't want to have to tell the whole sordid story in a crowded courtroom. I don't want to put my family through the heartache," she added.

"Even if it means prosecuting the guy?"

"I've heard of too many instances where criminals are let off on technicalities or they only serve a very small portion of their sentences before being freed. Why should I put myself through all that? I've already been a victim once. I don't want to become a victim of the legal system as well." Ellie was glad when their waiter showed up with the menus. She wanted to change the subject. Cutter seemed to sense it, because he didn't push. They ordered their meal and Cutter told her funny stories about the people on Erskine, including the time he and Clarence were called out to end a domestic dispute between Clovis and Dicker Henry, only to have Clovis turn on them with a garden rake. Ellie laughed until her eyes teared, until her sides ached and she was forced to ask him to stop so she could catch her breath, until Cutter was laughing just as hard and drawing stares from everybody around them.

His gaze softened and he covered her hand with his. "I like hearing you laugh, Ellie. It's good for my soul."

His expression was so tender, so sincere that Ellie was half afraid she would start crying again, this time because she was so moved. Cutter Beaumont, despite being a rogue and a flirt, despite that cocky devil-may-care demeanor, had touched her in a way that no other human being had come close to.

She was falling in love with him. That knowledge jolted her to the soles of her feet. For a moment all she could do was sit there and let the realization sink in. She loved him! She had come to the island a wounded, broken soul. Cutter had made her smile again. In just a short time, he'd made her glad that she had not died the night of her attack.

Ellie didn't even taste her food after that.

Halfway through dinner it started to rain. By the time the waiter picked up their plates and brought coffee, the wind and water were pounding the large plate-glass windows of the restaurant.

"Is the weather always so unpredictable?" Ellie asked, worrying that it wouldn't let up before they had to get back on the ferry to Erskine.

"This time of year it is. We have a lot of late-afternoon squalls, but they usually blow over." He paused. "I think this one is going to be a replay of last night." As if acting on cue, a flash of lightning lit up the sky.

"I didn't bring an umbrella," Ellie told him. "We'll get drenched walking back to the docks to catch the ferry."

He offered her a sheepish grin. "If the weather gets any worse, there won't be a ferry."

"How will we get back?"

"We won't. At least not tonight."

She was really concerned now and it showed in her wide-eyed expression. "What are we supposed to do, Cutter? Sleep on a park bench in the rain?"

"Calm down," he said, taking her hand and

squeezing it. "If it doesn't stop, we'll spend the night in town and go back in the morning."

"Spend the night where?"

"A hotel, where else? There's a perfectly good place across the street. It's sort of a bed and breakfast."

"I don't know, Cutter. What about my dog?"

"He'll be fine until you get back. Stop worrying. We'll order dessert and see what happens."

The weather got progressively worse as they ate their pecan pie with vanilla ice cream and drank more coffee. Finally, Cutter excused himself, telling her he was going to call the hotel and make sure they had rooms. When he returned he was smiling.

"I got us a suite with a king-size bed, how's that?"

"Can you afford it?"

He looked hurt. "A successful entrepreneur like myself? Of course I can afford it." He motioned for the check. It wasn't until after he'd paid it and thanked the waiter that he noticed how worried Ellie looked. His brows puckered in a thoughtful frown.

"Maybe I was being presumptuous to think you'd want to spend the night with me," he said. "It's just . . . after this morning." If she had looked anxious before, it was nothing compared to the expression on her face now. "Would you feel better if I asked for separate rooms?"

Ellie met his questioning gaze. "I'm sorry for being nervous. Things just sort of happened between us this morning. It wasn't planned."

His own expression grew tender. "It's going to kill me to say this, Ellie, but we don't have to make love. We could just hold each other if that'll make you more comfortable."

She thought of the scar she tried to keep hidden. "I don't have a change of clothes. What'll we sleep in?"

He shot her a disarming grin. "We've got our skivvies." Finally, he paused. "This isn't getting any easier for you, is it?"

She offered him a meek smile. "No, but I'll manage."

They left the restaurant a moment later, stood beneath the striped awning that marked the entrance, and waited for a lull in the rain. When there was none, Cutter grinned. "Looks like we're going to get wet, Ellie, honey."

Laughing, they dashed across the street—dodging a taxi and a delivery truck—and pushed through the front door of the hotel. Ellie noted the three-story structure resembled a country cottage. The small lobby was a cozy welcome from the weather with its cotton rugs and overstuffed furniture.

"You must be the gentleman who just called," the desk clerk said, excusing himself briefly, then returning with a clean towel for each of them. He smiled at Ellie as he handed her one. "I understand you live on Erskine and got caught in the storm." She nodded and thanked him as she tried to blot some of the excess water. "Your room is ready, Mr. Beaumont," he told Cutter, "and I just sent up some of the toiletry items you asked for."

"Thanks." Cutter stepped up to the desk to register.

An elevator took them to the third floor and their suite, a small apartment of rooms that was warmer and cozier than what one would find at a grander hotel. The king-size bed was a four-poster solid-mahogany piece with a quilted comforter.

"This must've cost you a fortune," Ellie told Cutter, knowing quality rooms when she saw them.

"Would you stop worrying about what it cost?" he said as he checked the bathroom. "Look, they have a towel-warming rack. Why don't you get out of those wet clothes and wrap up in one of them?"

Ellie was only too happy to get out of her damp things. She disappeared inside the bathroom, kicked off her heels and peeled off her wet pantyhose, then proceeded to undress. When she came out, wrapped in one of the giant bath towels, she found Cutter standing at the window. He turned and grinned when he saw her.

"Guess what? The rain is starting to let up."

"Do you want to go back?"

"Not really. Do you?"

She smiled, feeling more confident about the situation. After all, this was Cutter, the man she loved. "I'm okay now."

"Good. Mind if I get out of my wet things?"

"I saved one of the bath towels for you."

Cutter went into the bathroom and shucked out of his own clothes, then hung them over the shower curtain rack next to Ellie's so they could dry, trying not to notice her flimsy undergarments as he did so. When he entered the sitting room he found her on the sofa, legs tucked beneath her, watching television.

Ellie glanced up at him as he came into the room, then cut her eyes quickly to the TV set when she realized how little the towel covered when it came right down to it. And she would have had to be deaf, dumb, and blind not to notice what a striking figure Cutter Beaumont made in a bath towel. The mauve and mint green colors only emphasized his dark, leathery complexion. It took every ounce of willpower she had to keep from gawking at him.

"What're you watching?" he asked, taking a seat next to her.

She chuckled. "An old *Happy Days* rerun. Would you rather watch something else?"

"No, that's fine." Cutter stretched his long legs and propped them on the coffee table in front of him. As he watched the program, he was vaguely aware of Ellie watching him from time to time. She yawned, and he glanced over at her. "Tired?"

"A little." She adjusted herself on the sofa so that she was more comfortable.

Cutter reached for a throw pillow. "Here, put your head in my lap," he said.

She yawned again. "Are you sure?" At the moment, she would have given anything to go to bed, but the bedroom issue hadn't been settled yet, and she wasn't going to be the one to bring it up. Instead, she shifted to the other side and lay her head on the plump pillow in his lap. The big dinner she'd eaten had made her drowsy. She tried to keep her eyes open, but after a while it became too difficult.

Cutter was not sure when she had fallen asleep, but the gentle rise and fall of her chest told him she had drifted off at some point in the program. He gazed down at the dozing woman and smiled thoughtfully. She looked like a young girl with her legs drawn up, one fist tucked beneath her chin. But the body was definitely that of a woman. Her long legs were slim and shapely and everything a man could hope for.

"Ellie?" He nudged her gently. She stirred and mumbled something in her sleep but did not wake. Finally, he lifted her head slightly so he could get up, then picked her up and carried her toward the bedroom.

Startled, her eyes flew open. "Where are you taking me?"

"To bed, sweetheart. Don't worry, you're safe."

She relaxed and smiled. "I know."

Between the cool, crisp sheets, Ellie sighed dreamily and sought out Cutter's welcoming warmth. A deep feeling of peace stole over her as she tucked her head in the crook of his arm. At the same time, her body ached for his touch. She snuggled closer.

Cutter wasn't sure how long he lay there holding her, his body as stiff as a figure from one of those wax museums. The only thing he was sure of was the strong response his body was having to hers. Why did she have to feel so good in his arms? Why did her body have to fit so perfectly against his? He cursed the unfairness of it all. This was the first woman he'd cared about in a long time. Every instinct he had told him it was up to him to protect her. But the bulge at his thighs obviously hadn't come to terms with that fact.

"Cutter?"

His heart skipped a beat. "Yeah?"

"You're the best thing that's happened to me in a long time."

Damn, but she was sweet. He tightened his grip on her, knowing he would do anything to keep her safe. "Same here, babe," he said, then pressed a kiss against her forehead.

"I love you, Cutter."

A groan escaped his lips. "Dammit, Ellie!"

She jumped. "What?"

"How do you expect me to get any sleep *now*?" He didn't give her a chance to respond as he released her abruptly, swept the covers aside, and climbed out of the bed. He had to put some distance between them or die.

Ellie raised up, blinking at him in dazed confusion. "What'd I do?"

He sighed heavily. "Okay, it was bad enough we got stuck over here and had to stay in this hotel, but I told myself I could handle it. I'd be a gentleman if it killed me. Then, here you come prancing outta the bathroom in that skimpy towel—"

"I didn't prance, and the towel isn't skimpy."

"—but I said to myself, No problem, I can handle that too. But I can't handle it when you tell me you love me, because I don't have the foggiest idea what to do about it. I can't let myself get all hot and bothered over it, because I might get passionate, and that might frighten you. But if I *don't* do anything, you'll think it's because I'm turned off knowing you were raped. Jeez, Ellie, what the hell am I supposed to do?" Only then did he realize he'd been shouting.

Ellie lay there for a moment, stunned by what she'd put the man through. She was genuinely touched that he had tried so hard to do the right thing. At the same time, she realized they had reached the point where their relationship had to be resolved.

"I only have one thing to say to you, Cutter Beaumont," she replied haughtily.

He heard movement on the bed, but he couldn't see her clearly. "What?"

"This." She threw her towel at him as hard as she could.

It took a second for her meaning to sink in, and when it did, Cutter grinned and shrugged off his own towel. "Oh, Ellie," he said. His voice held a sensual note of warning. "You just bought yourself a whole lot of trouble."

Ellie's stomach quickened as the mattress dipped beneath his weight. The next thing she knew he was beside her—warm, naked, and hard.

He kissed her, gently at first, cupping her face with his palm. Then, as the kiss deepened, he made a hungry sound and ground his body against hers so there was no question as to what was on his mind.

Ellie felt small and vulnerable in his arms with his broad chest pressed against hers. Powerful legs tangled with hers beneath the covers—his lean and hair roughened, hers smooth and shapely. She felt his hardness at her thighs and knew he was thoroughly aroused. Would he stop if she asked? she wondered, and knew a split second of uneasiness. She was no match for him physically, and she knew it. But then he kissed her and she felt her insides turn to mush, and she knew that Cutter Beaumont would never have to force what was already his. And she knew there was no place else she'd rather be than in his arms.

When Cutter slipped his hands between Ellie's thighs, he let out another tortured moan. She was silky and wet. Using extreme care, he slipped his fingers past the swollen flesh. Ellie sighed and arched against his hand.

He swore under his breath and released her.

"Cutter?" She couldn't mask the disappointment in her voice.

He chuckled softly in the dark. "It's okay, baby. I've got something better." He scooted down on the bed, parted her thighs once more, then kissed her gently.

"Oh!" Ellie jumped as if she'd been touched with a live wire. Instinctively, she grasped his head, pressing him more firmly against her. His tongue was hot and probing; it teased and tantalized the tiny bud that housed her desire, then dipped inside her honeyed warmth. Ellie squirmed and quivered and rode wave after wave of pleasure.

Cutter raised up, positioned himself between her legs and sank into her softness. Her muscles pulsed and contracted around his sex, and he knew he was a dead man. He shuddered in her arms a moment later, chanting her name with sighs of release.

"I love you, Ellie."

When Ellie and Cutter stepped off the ferry the following morning, they found Rose and Franklin D. waiting for them. The little boy threw himself into Ellie's arms, sobbing uncontrollably. Ellie, who hadn't stopped smiling since she had awakened in Cutter's arms that morning, was suddenly jolted out of her euphoric state.

"Franklin D.? What's wrong?" She knelt beside him and held the child against her. He was trembling.

"Am I glad to see you," Rose said, shaking her head. "This boy kept me up all night pacing and crying."

Ellie gazed into the tearstained face, then raised her gaze to his mother. "What happened?"

"Well, Clarence told us Cutter had called and said you were staying on the mainland 'cause of the storm, but Franklin D. here wouldn't believe it. You know how he hates water and anything to do with water. He was convinced that old ferry went down with you on it and nothin' I said was going to change his mind." She nudged her son. "See there, Franklin D. I told you Miss Parks was going to be okay. Mr. Beaumont ain't about to let no harm come to her."

Ellie felt her heart turn in her chest as she gazed into Franklin D.'s tearful eyes. "Honey, I'm sorry I made you worry. Can you forgive me?"

He nodded, choked on a sob, then buried his face against her breasts. "Ell . . . ie," came a muffled sound.

A startled look passed through the group. Ellie wondered for a moment if she had imagined it. Taking the boy by the shoulders, she smiled into his face. "Franklin D., you just said my name."

"Oh, God," Rose said, kneeling beside her son as well. She looked dazed. She blinked and her eyes welled up with tears. She clasped her hands and turned her face to the heavens.

Cutter scratched his head. "I could use a drink."

Franklin D. beamed proudly. "Ell . . . ie Parks," he said, his eyes sparkling.

"Thank you, Lord!" Rose cried, beating her chest.

Cutter shook his head over the woman's emotional display. He grinned at the boy. "Welcome back, Franklin D." Then he glanced at Ellie. "See, we told you he'd talk when he got damn good 'n' ready."

Several days later Cutter and Ellie were admiring the first shoots in her garden. "I knew I could turn you into a farming woman," he said, slinging one arm over her shoulder.

"That's not all you've turned me into the past couple of days," she said, giving him a private smile.

He offered her a boyishly wicked grin. "Yes, well, you've become a brazen hussy too."

Ellie laughed softly and nuzzled her face against his neck. His flesh was warm and held a hint of the tangy after-shave he'd started wearing. "I like you better since you've taken up shaving on a regular basis," she said.

He chuckled. "Yes, well, I felt kind of guilty leaving whisker burns on your thighs."

"You're terrible!" she said, slapping his arm playfully.

"And don't you *ever* forget it." Without warning, he scooped her high in his arms, ignoring her squeals of protest. All he could think of was making love to her again. One of her shoes slipped off and fell to the ground, but Cutter didn't so much as slow down. "Take me to your bed, woman!" he said. "We haven't made love in hours." Ellie was still giggling when Cutter came to an abrupt halt.

"What's the matter, stud?" she said. Her smile faded when she saw the embarrassed look on his face, when she realized suddenly they were no longer alone. Ellie gasped out loud when she spotted Clarence Davis standing there, a blush staining his dark face. Standing beside him, frozen and erect as a statue, was her mother.

Twelve

At first, all Ellie could do was stare openmouthed at the petite woman. She was vaguely aware that Cutter had put her down and gone looking for her shoe.

"Mother, what on earth are *you* doing here?"

Nelda Parks drew herself up tightly. "Well, if you had bothered to call me as you'd promised, I wouldn't have had to make that miserable boat trip, then walk half a mile in sand up to my elbows in order to tell you." She paused and took in the two men with disdain. "Is there some place we can talk in private?"

"I was just leaving," Clarence said, looking relieved to have a reason to go. "Nice meetin' you, ma'am," he told the older woman. "Enjoy your visit to Erskine."

"That, young man, would take a miracle of the magnitude of the parting of the Red Sea."

"Yes ma'am." He nodded at Cutter and Ellie, rolled his eyes heavenward, and disappeared around the front of the house.

"What is it, Mother?" Ellie asked, certain the news had to be bad. "Is something wrong with Daddy? It's okay to talk in front of Cutter."

"Your father is hanging on by a thread as usual, thanks to your traipsing off to this deserted island. But that's not why I've come. The police have been calling for two days. They want you to come in to the station immediately."

"Why? What do they want?"

Nelda paused. "It's about that unpleasant business last year. They have someone who fits the man's description. They want you to come in and see if he's the one."

Ellie could feel the adrenaline gushing through her body as she pondered her mother's words. "Did you tell them I was out of town?"

"Yes, but it didn't do any good. A twelve-year-old girl was attacked last week and left for dead. When she regained consciousness, she said she thought she recognized the man as having worked in a convenience store in her area. The police picked him up, and he matches the description of the man who attacked you."

"Why didn't Daddy come with you?"

"I didn't want to drag him through this. He has enough problems of his own, what with his high blood pressure and all. He thinks I'm shopping in Charleston, but I have to be back tonight."

"Mother, I wish you'd stop treating Daddy like an invalid. The last time I saw him he looked wonderful."

"Only because I take such good care of him and see that he exercises and eats right. If it weren't for me, he'd be six feet under right now." She paused. "But I don't have time to argue with you about your father's poor physical condition. How long will it take you to pack?"

"Let's go inside and cool off first," Ellie suggested, hoping to buy a little time. She had no desire to go back with her mother. "You, too, Cutter," she added, suspecting there were at least a half dozen places he'd rather be at the moment.

Inside, Ellie poured them each a glass of iced tea and made the introductions. "Mr. Beaumont is the sheriff and mayor of Erskine," Ellie said.

"And the saloon owner," he added.

Nelda Parks offered him a stiff smile. "How nice for you. Have you been long on the island?"

Cutter could tell she didn't like him worth a cuss. Well, he didn't much care for her either. "Ten years," he said. "I've got me a mobile home on the other side of those trees." That oughta cock her pistol, he thought. She had snob written all over her.

"Imagine that," Nelda said with the enthusiasm one might offer someone who'd just inherited swampland.

Giving her that cocky, insolent smile of his, Cutter pulled a chair from the table, turned it around, and straddled it. He took a swig of tea and wiped his mouth on the back of his hand. She was there to take Ellie back to Savannah. In his mind that was even worse than being a snob. "You like coon dogs, Miz Parks?"

She offered him a tight smile. "I wouldn't know, Mr. Beaumont. I've never seen one."

Ellie stepped forward. "Cutter, could I speak with you in private for a moment?"

"Well, I got a whole mess of 'em out back," he went on as though he hadn't heard. "You'll have to come by sometime for a cold beer, and I'll show 'em to you."

"Cutter?" Ellie nudged him hard this time and almost sent him toppling off his chair.

"Would you excuse us, Miz Parks?" he said. "It seems your daughter has urgent business with me."

"What do you think you're doing!" Ellie demanded the moment they were alone in her bedroom.

There was humor in his dark eyes. "Being my usual charming self, what else?"

"You're acting like a fool!"

He rested his hands on her shoulders. "Ellie, I once told you I'd never use force on a woman, but now I realized I lied. I'll do anything short of murder to get your mother off this island."

"Look, you don't have to like her, but she's still my mother."

"I'm so thankful you're different from her." He chuckled as he said it, but after a moment, the smile faded. He shoved his hands deep in his pockets. "You're going to have to go back with her, you know." As much as he hated to admit it, as much as he wished her mother had never come for her, he knew she had to go.

Ellie almost cringed. "Why?"

"You know why, babe. You've got to see if he's the one."

Ellie turned away from him. "He won't be the one. I've been through this before. I get myself all worked up, then it turns out it's not him after all. I don't want to go through it anymore, Cutter."

He grasped her by the arm and turned her around. "What about that twelve-year-old girl lying in the hospital, Ellie? If he's the one, you've got to see that they put him away so he can't hurt anyone else. If you can't do it for yourself, at least do it for the girl."

Ellie felt the sting of tears. "That's not fair, Cutter. I've already been through enough. Why do you have to try and make me feel guilty?"

"Because I care about you. And I don't want you to carry this with you for the rest of your life. How will you live with yourself if they have to let him go and he strikes again? What if he actually succeeds in killing someone next time?"

"Then go with me." Her eyes implored him.

He touched her face. "I can't, baby. I've got a business to run. This is something you have to do by yourself." He saw that his words had hurt her, and the look in her eyes sent a raw pain through his own heart. "I once told you I didn't want you to use me or this island as your hiding place," he said softly. "I want you to feel safe in my arms, but I also want you to know that you're capable of protecting yourself if you have to. You have to do this, Ellie."

She gazed back at him. "You don't care about me. If you did, you'd never try to send me away. You wouldn't let me face this alone." It hurt that he could let her go so easily, when she had finally learned to trust and give her heart. It was a direct slap in the face. "What's wrong, Cutter, are you bored now that you've gotten what you wanted from me?"

"You know that's not true." He was prevented from answering when Nelda Parks tapped on the door.

"Ellie, we need to get started," she said.

Cutter looked at Ellie. "Go ahead and get your

things packed, and I'll take care of the house and the dog until you come back."

"I'm *not* coming back," she snapped.

He didn't so much as bat an eye. "I guess that's pretty much up to you." He started for the door. "You can reach me by phone, Ellie. Anytime."

The look she gave him told him she'd die first. "Please ask Clarence to come by in an hour," she said woodenly. "He'll need to carry my things to the dock."

He was being dismissed. Cutter glanced at Nelda Parks and saw the victorious look in her eyes. "See you around, Ellie," he said, then left the room. He loaded Ellie's dog into the back of his Jeep a moment later and drove away.

The police station was exactly as she remembered: crowded and noisy and smelling of cigarette smoke and burned coffee. "Hello, Sergeant Lewis," Ellie said, speaking to the bald man whom she had dealt with from the beginning. He held out a beefy fist, and she shook it. "It's been a while."

"Miss Parks, nice to see you again." Frank Lewis smiled. His teeth held the telltale stains of too much coffee and nicotine. "I'm sorry we had to interrupt your vacation, but we might have something this time." He paused. "You okay?"

Ellie offered him the closest thing she had to a smile. "Let's just get it over with."

"I understand." He picked up his phone, punched a button, then spoke into it quietly. When he hung up, he stood and cupped one fist beneath Ellie's elbow. "Let's go."

The next thing she knew, Ellie was sitting in a

chair in front of a large window. She fidgeted with her hands and found her palms damp. Although she had been there before, the situation never failed to unnerve her.

"Relax, hon," the sergeant said. "Remember, they can't see you."

Ellie nodded, and the door in the next room was shoved open and a group of six men herded inside and ordered against a wall. She studied the first three men carefully. Nothing registered. As the fourth man paused and turned, she gasped out loud. "Oh my God!" All the color drained from her face. She closed her eyes tightly and swiveled around in her chair, putting her back to the glass.

Sergeant Lewis snapped his head around just in time to see Ellie collapse. He grabbed her. "Steady now, Miss Parks. Are you all right?"

"It's him," she said, her voice sounding like a croak.

"Which one?"

"Number four."

"Are you sure?"

"Yes."

"Take a drink of water, Miss Parks."

Ellie opened her eyes and took the glass from him. She was shaking so badly, she sloshed the water over the side. The sergeant had to help her get it to her lips. He waited until she had drunk half the water before speaking.

"You're going to have to take a better look, Miss Parks."

Tears filled her eyes. "I can't. Besides, I know it's him. If you'll look closely, you'll see there's a fairly wide gap between his front teeth. And did you look for the tattoo I told you about? It's on his left hand. I saw it when he put his hand over my mouth."

"Describe the tattoo for me."

"I already did. Months ago."

"Do it again, Miss Parks. These are serious charges. We have to be sure."

She swallowed. "It's a heart with an arrow through it." She was trembling all over now. "Can I go now?"

"After you take one more look. You're going to have to face him in court anyway. Might as well get used to looking at his ugly mug."

Silent tears slid down her face. "No."

"What do you mean, no?" the sergeant demanded. "You're not going to back out on us now, are you?" He grabbed Ellie and shook her slightly. "Would you like for me to tell you what he did to that twelve-year-old girl, Miss Parks?"

"No, please—" She choked out the words. "We don't know if the same man raped her. We don't know—"

"Yes, we do. The victim said the man worked at a convenience store near her house. She remembered him from the tattoo."

Panic filled Ellie's throat. She sat there for a moment, torn as to what to do. She could not imagine a young girl going through the same horrors she had and living to tell it. Finally, taking a deep breath, she turned toward the window once more. The men in the lineup were ordered to turn left and right so she could get a clear view. When the fourth man stepped closer to the window, she grabbed the sergeant's hand and held it tightly, unaware that her nails were biting into the man's flesh. Finally, the men were dismissed and

Ellie found herself looking into an empty room once more.

"Well, Miss Parks?" the sergeant asked in a gently voice as he squeezed her hand in reassurance.

"I'm positive it's him," she said, her voice little more than a whisper. "I won't forget that face as long as I live."

"Are you prepared to do something about it?"

Ellie knew what that meant. Her life would be turned topsy-turvy. She would be forced to sit through court and stare at her attacker every day until the jury made their decision. She would have to relive her attack. She knew it would be easier to just walk away and never look back.

Then she thought of the girl whose life had been changed forever. She thought of her own life, how she'd spent the last year, simply because some monster had attacked her.

"I'll do whatever I have to do," she said at last.

Ellie went back to work the following week. Although she was glad to see her old friends and office staff, the excitement she'd once had over her job was gone. It no longer challenged her.

She was bored and restless.

And she missed Cutter, not only what they'd had together, but what they could have had. She wondered if he was caring for her little garden as he'd promised, whether he was taking good care of Duke. She thought of Franklin D., whom she'd written a letter to because she hadn't had time to say good-bye; of Rose, who had quickly become a good friend. She thought of the letters Cutter had sent that she had tossed in the trash can without bothering to read. He had let her down when she'd needed him most.

And then one day she pulled up in front of her condo and found Cutter Beaumont sitting on her front steps. She blinked once, twice, and again, thinking she surely must be imagining things. He stood and walked to her car, then opened the door.

"Are you going to get out?" he asked.

Half afraid her legs would not support her, Ellie stepped out of the car and waited for him to close the door. "What are you doing here?" she demanded, trying not to notice how good he looked in his tight jeans and floral shirt. The straw hat was absent, but he still looked like the worst kind of rogue.

"I came to see you."

"So, you've seen me. Good-bye." She turned to go.

Cutter grabbed her by the arm. "Not so fast, Miz Parks," he drawled in that lazy tone of his that always had the power to curl her toes. "How come you didn't answer my letters?"

"Because I have nothing to say to you."

"You didn't tell me your phone number was unlisted."

"That's right, I didn't."

"You're not going to make this any easier on me, are you?" he said with a slight smile. When she didn't answer, he dropped the smile and his look softened. "I'm sorry, Ellie. Can you forgive me?"

Her bottom lip trembled.

"I was wrong, baby. I should have come with you."

She sighed and looked at him. "You were right. It was something I needed to take care of myself."

His eyes caressed her face. She looked tired. He wanted to kick himself for not coming back with her. "And did you?"

"Yes. Court isn't scheduled for a few months, but I'm prepared to testify."

"So what are you going to do with yourself in the meantime?" he asked.

"Live my life, what else?"

"Here in Savannah?"

"Where else?"

"I was sort of hoping you'd come back to Erskine with me."

She had not expected that one. She snapped her head up, thinking she would find that teasing glint in his. He looked serious. "Why would I do that?"

"Because I love you, Ellie. And because you love me. We'd make a good team, you and me. Besides, I need you. I can't be sheriff and mayor and operate all those businesses by myself."

"So you're offering me a job?" she asked stiffly.

He ducked his head. "Not exactly, no. I'm sort of asking you to marry me."

She sucked her breath in sharply. "Marry you?"

He met her gaze. "I just threw in the other stuff to make it sound more appealing."

It took every ounce of willpower she had to keep from laughing out loud. "What makes you think I'd be willing to move to a deserted island and live in a mobile home with a man who seldom shaves and owns coon dogs?" She crossed her arms and tapped one toe impatiently. "And how would I ever break the news to my mother?"

"We could tell her you're pregnant and have no choice. Anyway, we don't *have* to live in a mobile home. We'll ask Miss Simms's son to sell us her place. I'm sure he'd be willing to do it, since his mother's never going to get out of that nursing home." He paused. "We can work all that out, Ellie. I just can't stand the thought of going back without you. I'm willing to do almost anything. I'll even take you to the mainland for shopping and dinner so you don't feel stuck on that island."

She wondered if he had any idea how sexy and dear he looked standing in her front yard trying to convince her to marry him. She had never felt trapped on the island. On the contrary, she had found all she'd needed. "I don't know if you'd be good marriage material, Cutter," she said after a moment.

"I wouldn't be here if I didn't think I could make it work for us, Ellie. You're the first woman I've ever met that really needed me and saw hope in what I am. I like who I am when I'm with you. I want to take care of you. I want us to have children just as soon as you learn to cook." When she frowned, he went on quickly. "But I'm not opposed to spending time in the kitchen as well. I'm not here because I need someone to clean and cook for me. I think we could have a good life together if you'll give me a chance."

"I have to come back in a few months for court."

"And next time I'll come with you. I promise."

"It's not going to be easy."

"I don't expect it to. But as long as we're together, we can get through it. I won't let you down again."

With his heart in his eyes, Cutter reached for her. "Ellie, you're the first woman I've trusted my heart to in a long time. I can go back to Erskine and live without you, but I have no desire to. Nothing really seems important to me without you there to share it." Ellie stepped into the circle of his arms, and he pulled her close. "Say you'll marry me, sweetheart. The guys at the saloon bet five hundred bucks you wouldn't. We'll have enough to pay for the honeymoon." He grinned.

She chuckled softly, her eyes bright with happiness. He had never looked more like a rogue. How could she *not* agree to marry him, when he had taught her to laugh again.

And to love.

THE EDITOR'S CORNER

Soon we'll be rushing into the holiday season, and we have some special LOVESWEPT books to bring you good cheer. Nothing can put you in a merrier mood than the six fabulous romances coming your way next month.

The first book in our lineup is **PRIVATE LESSONS** by Barbara Boswell, LOVESWEPT #582. Biology teacher Gray McCall remembers the high school student who'd had a crush on him, but now Elissa Emory is all grown up and quite a knockout. Since losing his family years ago, he hadn't teased or flirted with a woman, but he can't resist when Elissa challenges him to a sizzling duel of heated embraces and fiery kisses. Extracurricular activity has never been as tempting as it is in Barbara's vibrantly written romance.

With **THE EDGE OF PARADISE,** LOVESWEPT #583, Peggy Webb will tug at your heartstrings—and her hero will capture your heart. David Kelly is a loner, a man on the run who's come looking for sanctuary in a quiet Southern town. Still, he can't hide his curiosity—or yearning—for the lovely woman who lives next door. When he feels the ecstasy of being in Rosalie Brown's arms, he begins to wonder if he has left trouble behind and finally found paradise. A superb love story from Peggy!

Only Jan Hudson can come up with a heroine whose ability to accurately predict the weather stems from her once having been struck by lightning! And you can read all about it in **SUNNY SAYS,** LOVESWEPT #584. Kale Hoaglin is skeptical of Sunny Larkin's talent, and that's a problem since he's the new owner of the small TV station where Sunny works as the weather reporter. But her unerring predictions—and thrilling kisses—soon make a believer of him. Jan continues to delight with her special blend of love and laughter.

Please give a rousing welcome to new author Deborah Harmse and her first novel, **A MAN TO BELIEVE IN,** LOVESWEPT #585. This terrific story begins when Cori McLaughlin attends a costume party and catches the eye of a wickedly good-looking pirate. Jake Tanner can mesmerize any woman, and Cori's determined not to fall under his spell. But to be the man in her life, Jake is ready to woo her with patience, persistence, and passion. Enjoy one of our New Faces of 1992!

Michael Knight feels as if he's been **STRUCK BY LIGHTNING** when he first sees Cassidy Harrold, in LOVESWEPT #586 by Patt Bucheister. A mysterious plot of his matchmaking father brought him to England, and with one glimpse of Cassidy, he knows he'll be staying around for a while. Cassidy has always had a secret yen for handsome cowboys, and tangling with the ex–rodeo star is wildly exciting, but can she be reckless enough to leave London behind for his Montana home? Don't miss this enthralling story from Patt!

Tonya Wood returns to LOVESWEPT with **SNEAK,** #587, and this wonderful romance has definitely been worth waiting for. When Nicki Sharman attacks the intruder in her apartment, she thinks he's an infamous cat burglar. But he turns out to be Val Santisi, the rowdy bad boy she's adored since childhood. He's working undercover to chase a jewel thief, and together they solve the mystery of who's robbing the rich—and steal each other's heart in the process. Welcome back, Tonya!

FANFARE presents four spectacular novels that are on sale this month. Ciji Ware, the acclaimed author of *Romantic Times* award-winner **ISLAND OF THE SWANS,** delivers